"C'mere. We do this accurately, or we don't do it at all."

Martha pushed off the ropes and positioned herself against a corner post.

"I hadn't laughed, cracked a smile—none of it—in weeks," he recalled, advancing toward her in a few careful steps. As he had four years ago, he gripped the top rope on her left and the one on her right. "And you told the lamest-ass joke I'd ever heard."

"It was beautiful, your laugh," she whispered, pensive, her expression drawn in a frown. "So rough. Unexpected. I felt it everywhere. All over me."

"Then you put your hands on me, Martha."

She coiled her fingers over his forearms, her nails imprinting on his jacket. "I wanted to make you feel the heat I felt just being near you."

Past and present collided as her palms skimmed his arms. He'd lived this moment before, only now there was more. More sizzle in his blood at the brush of her hands on his collar. More urgency in the crash of their bodies....

Books by Lisa Marie Perry

Harlequin Kimani Romance

Night Games
Midnight Play
Just for Christmas Night

LISA MARIE PERRY

thinks an imagination's a terrible thing to ignore. So is a good cappuccino. After years of college, customer service gigs and a career in caregiving, she at last gave in to buying an espresso machine and writing to her imagination's desire. Lisa Marie lives in America's heartland, and she has every intention of making the Colorado mountains her new stomping grounds. She drives a truck, enjoys indie rock, collects Medieval literature, watches too many comedies, has a not-so-secret love for lace and adores rugged men with a little bit of nerd.

Just FOR CHRISTMAS NIGHT

Lisa Marie Perry

HARLEQUIN® KIMANI™ ROMANCE

For Ruby—

*Because you volunteered to be my angel
when I needed one.*

Recycling programs
for this product may
not exist in your area.

ISBN-13: 978-0-373-86383-9

Just for Christmas Night

Copyright © 2014 by Lisa Marie Perry

For questions and comments about the quality of this book please contact us
at CustomerService@Harlequin.com.

Printed in U.S.A.

Dear Reader,

Sleigh bells. Crisp, pine-scented breezes. Mistletoe. These are all tiny somethings that I adore at Christmastime. Beyond that is what I treasure most: *hope*. During my journey with *Just for Christmas Night*, I lost someone who was precious to me—and I spent countless hours grieving. In myriad ways, I still am. But I believe in little miracles, in hidden blessings and holiday magic. I believe that on the other side of the unknown and the unexpected, of changes and surprises, are hope and opportunity.

The wildest of the Blue daughters, freewheeling flirt Martha, has plans for herself. But as her life jumps the rails, she gets a spectacular holiday surprise of her own: brooding boxing champ Joaquin Ryder. Watching Martha and Joaquin figure each other out showed me just how steamy the holidays can be!

Here's to hope, opportunity and little miracles.

XOXO

Lisa Marie Perry

Chapter 1

Gone too long...

Miami was the place he had depended on for the past four years. It was his refuge...where he slept. Partied. Trained. Decompressed after championships. Lived as a prince who finally knew the vices and virtues of luxury, yet refused to quit fighting dirty with his fists, like the pauper he'd been for most of his existence.

But Florida wasn't where Joaquin "Sinner" Ryder belonged. Las Vegas—no, Ryder's Boxing Club, the single-level concrete gym built on the labors of friendship, favors and six-packs of beer, with the hands of men whose aged Polaroid photographs were stuck with tape, tacks and wads of chewing gum to a chipped cork bulletin board in the lobby—had possession of his heart.

Without the place that anchored his entire damn life, without the place his soul's compass had always pointed toward, he'd begun to drift. Now wasn't the time to veer off the narrow road to victory. He was a man whose wealth could satisfy his greed, but he couldn't afford to let the international hype surrounding his upcoming pay-per-view fight, his ex-fiancée's malice or the pressure to remain America's undefeated super middleweight champ get to him.

So he'd found his way back to his uncle's gym, where it had all begun. He was making the boxing ring his own again. Here, he found his greatest strengths and laid down his every vulnerability.

In this gym, he followed the establishment's cardinal rule: no lies, no bullshit. The truth was rarely a pretty thing, and the men who trained and sweated and mingled with triumph and defeat inside these walls never expected it to be.

Which was why he felt no stirring of remorse or apology when he let out a gritty curse and motioned for his uncle, Jules, to drop his hands. "Got company," he ground out, making a concentrated effort to relax his stance in spite of the tension pouring over his spine like liquid lead. It wasn't the tension of channeling his thoughts, instincts, emotions and maneuvers into a trainer-versus-student session with a man who never gave less than his strongest assault in the ring.

This sensation was foreign, exotic, and had everything to do with the woman who knew she had no right to be in his arena but was invading it anyway.

"Company? Eh, what the hell you talkin' about?" Jules jabbed his chest, his eyes alight with camaraderie Joaquin couldn't force himself to imitate, then snapped up his chin at his sons, who'd been circling the ring, observing. "The Blues are as good as family 'round here."

Tor immediately took to the ring, loose-limbed and ready to remove his father's battered boxing gloves, which could've been as old as Tor himself. His younger brother, Othello, three years past Joaquin's thirty-three years, remained stationed at one of the posts, looking past Marshall Blue to the waiflike woman trailing in his shadow.

Beautiful destruction. That was Martha. Spontaneity and lust and complication packaged in a little-bit-of-nothing dress that appeared too flimsy for a fifty-degree December day and cemented Joaquin's belief that he would never see a sexier pair of legs.

You don't want to tangle with her, man. The word of caution was skating around on his tongue, but he clenched his teeth. For four years it had served him well to see no Martha, hear no Martha. Getting involved, even just to advise his Casanova cousin to direct his curiosity else-where, would do him no good. Wild, unwise and as deep as a puddle of dog piss she might seem, but Martha knew too much. Always had.

"Big man! Came this way to see Vegas's prince?" Face sweaty, hands taped, Jules hopped off the platform and cut across the room to shake Marshall's hand.

Topping six and a half feet, strapped with muscles and both blessed and cursed with a hard face that set strangers on edge, Jules was the harshest opponent Joaquin had ever sparred with. Being rescued from a crack house and brought into the man's household a skinny, self-conscious kid with a stutter had been a terrifying hell with two older cousins to whip his ass, until Jules had taught him to de-fend himself…to fight for respect.

Jules rivaled Marshall Blue in height and bulk, but "big man" referred to Marshall's status. Damn near a baron in this city, he had social influence and a Midas touch when it came to wealth. Investing in BioCures West Energy Corp., one of the country's most prosperous power companies—a move that had doubled his net worth—wasn't enough for Blue, who regarded everything in his world as a competi-tion. He and his wife had purchased the city's NFL fran-chise, and if the sports section of the *Las Vegas Sun* was right, the Las Vegas Slayers were looking at going into play-offs with a near-perfect season.

One loss. That was a luxury Joaquin didn't have. He was undefeated, and was bent on staying undefeated. That was what coming home to Las Vegas, reconnecting with his roots, was about.

"He's gonna be ready for Eliáš Brazda next month. He'll make us proud at MGM Grand," Jules assured Marshall, as if Joaquin wasn't pacing the platform several feet away. "He's looking good. His eyes. They've got passion."

Joaquin spared Martha a fraction of a sideways glance

as he crossed to the corner of the ring where his cousin Othello now waited with a towel and a bottle of water.

"She's grown up." Othello reached to assist with Joaquin's gloves. "What is she—twenty-two?"

"Twenty-three."

Flexing his fingers, Joaquin took the water but ignored the towel despite the rivulets of sweat traveling down his bare chest. The residue of jet lag from last night's flight from Florida to Nevada had bogged him down this morning, so when he'd showered and thrown on a hoodie and athletic shorts, he hadn't given two craps about style— only the basics.

He didn't bother to zip the black hooded sweatshirt as he assessed Martha. The details struck him down. Skin the color of pale caramel. Gilded brown hair in thousands of springy spirals that would feel weightless bunched in his fists. Cleft chin that made him weak to distraction when she frowned. Plump lips that could whisper the sweetest venom.

Her eyes—dark as a night abandoned by the moon and stars—were different. Shuttered. Guarded. Protected.

He knew her—closely, intimately, tragically. To pretend he didn't was a lie he lived with every day.

Yanking the hood over his head, Joaquin turned back to his cousin. "Gotten older, yeah. We all did."

"Get the sweat out of your eyes and *look*, bruh." Othello swore under his breath, shaking his head. "If I suffocated in those tits right now, I'd die a happy, horny man."

"Maybe if you'd paid more attention to either of your ex-wives' tits, instead of other women's, you'd be a happy married man."

"First wife told me I was perfect until the day we said 'I do.' Then she started a campaign to change me. Second wife wanted a baby to 'strengthen' our marriage, miscarried, went all crazy-ass, then ate her way to three bills."

Othello shrugged. "My appreciation for the female sex wasn't the problem."

It was, if that *appreciation* was what the first wife had wanted to change or the reason the second wife had hoped a baby would keep their marriage intact.

"Just know that Martha doesn't need your appreciation, Othello."

"But that's what this gym is missing. Women like her."

"Any woman's welcome here if she wants to learn how to fight. I don't think Uncle Jules has changed his mind on that. The fight is what this place is about. Why do you think it's still standing after forty-something years?"

"Too stubborn to burn to the ground."

Joaquin's eyebrows furrowed under the edge of his hood. "What the hell?"

"A joke. Just a joke. Get your head out of the ring once in a while. In the land of the living people jive around." Othello exited the ring and smiled at Martha in a way that revitalized Joaquin's need to crush something with his fists.

His cousins took off for beers and a card game in the lounge—the section of Jules's gym that had been completely upgraded after Joaquin's first big-money fight had earned enough profit to make his uncle-slash-trainer a financially comfortable man in his own right.

Martha approached the ring, wrapping her hands around the bottom rope. There hadn't been so little distance between them in four slow-motion years. She'd trusted him then, and he'd used that trust to hurt her.

When a man was against the ropes and had only one desperate shot, he had to take it.

"The prodigal play-boyfriend returns."

Play-boyfriend. It had been her nickname for him when he'd been a teenager and she a coltish chatterbox, admiring him as though he were an older brother but convinced that she loved him. If he hadn't been so focused on being her father's protégé, and sopping up the blessing of being welcomed into a family with riches he'd never dreamed of, he could've avoided tearing Martha apart.

He could've avoided hurting her in a way that froze solid any affection his bastard heart could hold.

"I stayed off your territory, as you'd asked."

Joaquin hadn't asked—he'd given her enough hostility to remove any doubt that she'd come back to this gym.

"You're here now." The words scraped his tongue like sandpaper on gravel. The water offered no relief, but he drank anyway.

"Pop and I have a lunch date. This pit stop was his idea—I had no say."

"Could've told him no."

"Could've told him a lot of things, Joaquin."

Joaquin screwed the cap onto his water bottle, bent to set it on the stool in exchange for his gloves. "Sounds like a threat."

"But it isn't," she said solemnly, reaching through the ropes impatiently for the gloves. When he crouched and let her help him secure them, she pressed those luscious lips together before speaking again. "Your four years in Miami haven't changed the fact that Marshall and Tem consider you the son they never had. Their admiration, pride, respect—you have it. I'm not vindictive enough to take that away from them. Or you."

"You don't owe me protection. If they ever ask me whether we crossed the line, I'm going to tell them the truth. I won't lie."

"Noble of you. But what I owe you is a word of gratitude." Was that sarcasm or sincerity? "What you said to me that night left an impression. What happened—worse, what *could've* happened—then was as much my fault as it was yours."

"As much? Sixty-forty," he said, straightening and then for a moment sliding his eyes shut against the recollection.

Martha had been so persuasive, unraveling every strand of his resistance…

She tugged on the rope, and the guard over her emotions slipped. *Apologize to me. Give me back the dignity you stole.*

Those words she would never tell him, but she didn't have to because he'd already found them in her eyes. A boxing ring could make anyone vulnerable—even Martha Blue.

"How are you, Martha?"

"You know me—every day's a party."

"Marshall," he said to the man who'd begun as his mentor but was now his friend, "if you want to talk, get a couple of punch pads and get in the ring. Can't take a break—got a fight to train for."

Martha released the rope as her father accepted a pair of pads and took to the corner steps in a dark suit complete with gold cuff links and a handkerchief that probably cost more than the materials purchased to build this gym's original structure. "I'm going to the lounge. Tor and Othello might have something interesting to say. Escort me, Jules?"

Joaquin's gaze followed her. Silently he warned her against getting in over her head because she wasn't a kid anymore and his cousins—one married and the other twice divorced—had noticed.

But she didn't turn back.

"Good to have you home," Marshall said, raising his hands and gesturing for Joaquin to punch.

"Being in Vegas is good for my mind." Joaquin focused less on speed and more on crisp jabs and technique. "Fight night is what it's about, but there are people who helped me get to this point. I'm going to make time for them."

"Mean that?"

"'No lies, no bullshit,'" he said, quoting the sign mounted over the gym's exit. The words governed his life. Anyone who wanted a spot in his circle had to live by those words; he refused to tolerate neither lies nor bullshit.

Marshall's bald pate glowed under the white-gold lighting as he nodded. "I can appreciate that. When Charlotte and Danica met you and brought you to the family, and I got you started in business and investing, you offered to reciprocate my wife's and my kindness."

An offer Marshall had brushed off with a jovial smile on a face that, of a certainty, had limited experience smiling. *Just make damn sure none of those fights knocks the knowledge out of your head, son.*

But Joaquin knew Marshall was a man who never forgave a debt and never forgot a favor extended to him.

"Christmas is coming up. I want peace in my family, and there's a way you can help me achieve that."

Jab. "How?" *Jab, retreat, jab.* "I heard about what went down with Charlotte this past summer in Mount Charleston. And I heard Danica resigned as GM. Neither of those problems has anything to do with me, my friend."

"Right. I'm in this ring to talk about Martha."

Joaquin missed his target and swore. Rolling his shoulders, he resumed with two words echoing in his brain. *Concentration. Accuracy.*

"I'm accepting that offer, Joaquin." Marshall lowered his arms, and Joaquin halted. "My daughters have embarrassed me, kept secrets, sacrificed the integrity of our team and the game to go after what they wanted. But at least Charlotte and Danica know what they want. They know who they are now. They grew up to be strong, decisive women. I can't help but treasure that."

There it was again—vulnerability. This was a father's plea. Joaquin couldn't imagine—would never know—what it meant to love someone unconditionally even as they devastated you and what you valued most.

Martha's laughter, entwined with Othello's, rang out

from the lounge. Joaquin felt his jaw tighten with envy he didn't want.

"The Slayers are heading to the play-offs with a better record than the team has ever had. We withstood Charlotte's training camp indiscretion in the preseason. We're still getting past Danica's choice to give up the general manager position to have a relationship with our quarterback. There's no room for screwups in the postseason."

"You're assuming it's Martha's turn to get on the media's bad side, Marshall?"

"She's already there. Not because she made an unpopular decision for some personal convictions, but because she's careless."

"C'mon. What are you saying?"

"Businessmen make assessments. I've assessed that she's a liability—bad for my franchise. What she needs is the right person to get through to her."

That's not me. If I was unselfish enough to tell you why, you'd agree.

"Give her some of your time. Distract her. Just through the play-offs, then Tem and I will redirect her attention."

"Fire her ass, you mean?"

"Martha's sabotaging her reputation, and she'll drag the Blue name, the team's name, down with her." Marshall's frown deepened the creases on his face. "Unless you stop her."

Chapter 2

It was her own fault.

If Martha were in the mood to be fair, she'd admit that no one had coerced her to give her mother access to her house.

Blame it on the season of giving, but she'd been in particularly generous spirits when she'd gifted her parents and sisters with spare keys on Cartier key chains. Over Pinot Grigio and shrimp appetizers that she'd prepared with her own two flawlessly manicured hands—after she'd ruined the first couple of attempts and had resorted to phoning a chef friend who'd talked her through the recipe, because come hell or high water she'd prove that she could accomplish *something*—she'd shared with her family the new entry code to the mansion's security gate and with a big, fat grin had encouraged, "Visit anytime you'd like!"

Oh, how she wished she'd choked on the Pinot Grigio… an appetizer…her own spit. Anything to intercept the words she had instantly regretted saying. After twenty-three years of crawling through life beneath her parents' power, reputation and intimidating existence, she should know exactly how Marshall and Temperance Blue operated.

An unlimited, unrestricted invitation to her house had been a way to soften the impact of living on her own. But like a Band-Aid placed atop the carnage of nuclear destruction, what good did it serve?

Baby steps toward independence, they might be. But passing up the frills of a private wing in a crème-de-la-crème Las Vegas mansion in favor of her sister's hand-me-down divorce settlement property plus a position as a youth crisis center volunteer was the perfect route to rescue.

When a girl needed to save herself, she couldn't always be choosy. Even Martha, who'd enjoyed the world's finest delights, had come to grips with that. She had numbed herself to insults that rolled off her satin-smooth back as easily as she rolled off her favorite silk sheets. A partyer extraordinaire whom the American media criticized while obsessively tracking the clubs she frequented, the trends she set, the booze she tasted and the men who lured her close on the dance floor, she was cognizant to the fact that life—no matter how trussed up in glamour—was never perfect.

She did appreciate that her sister's place was beyond spacious and had a turret just perfect for Martha, who'd proudly brought along her beloved storybook collection to college in New York.

For someone who screwed up as often as Martha, it helped to have a happy ending lying around.

Of course, there wasn't a fairy tale within reach now, as she scrambled about the sitting room for something to adequately cover her ass. Partially sleep-addled, partially hungover and partially pissed off that she'd managed only two gulps of steaming caffeine before her mother had barged into the house at such a cruelly early hour, she was struggling to get her brain to function. It didn't help that Tem's anger was rising to impressive heights with each shriek.

Tem pointed at Martha with the end of her spare key. "This is a new low point! You're standing around naked with some man I've never met—and I'm sure your father hasn't met him, either."

Martha climbed onto the sofa, sinking her feet into the cushions, peering behind the leather beast for her shoes. She'd kicked them off last night and couldn't recall where they'd landed. As for her jeans, this morning she'd spilled bourbon on them while transporting the remnants of last night's refreshments into the kitchen, and had peeled them off and dropped them into the sink to soak. "I'm not naked, Ma. Just pants-less, if you will."

"I won't."

Martha's already paper-thin patience dissolved. In deliberate, serpent-like movements, she stepped off the sofa and draped herself over the cushions, slithering her slim body across the cognac-brown leather. Clothed in panties and a baggy sweater, she was reasonably covered except for her exposed legs and feet—which were, in fact, the physical assets she most admired.

Attractive, they were. But Martha was grateful for their strength…that her legs' length could make her always stand tall even when she shrank beneath feelings of insignificance, that her feet carried her to freedom, whether she was dancing from one club to another on a sleepless Vegas night or running away from conflict.

But the mere suggestion that the lone man in the room was the reason for Martha's current *pants-less* state was doing strange things to her mother's disposition.

Tem was normally a gust of refreshing, perfumed air. Only family, or people acquainted with her inside the proprietary walls of the Blues' NFL franchise's front office, were aware of the hell storm that slumbered in the shadows of her personality. A thoroughly angry Tem was not someone to bait.

She had graduated from pointing the business end of the house key to viciously jabbing it in the air. In the direction of the six-foot slab of good-looking testosterone standing between Tem and her youngest daughter.

Clearly, Gideon Crane, who'd still been sprawled across the sofa asleep when the Teminator had come charging into the house, had no clue what was going on. He knew only the truth—that he, Martha and the others had spent a platonic night together, drifting to sleep after the second helping of bourbon ice cream and Candyman's first kill.

The night had wound up an effective distraction for Martha, who'd wanted to distance herself from the messy feelings that had resurfaced when she'd walked into Jules Ryder's gym yesterday. Sports media pursued the next-to-perfect Las Vegas Slayers, but it also pursued Joaquin. To the press, he was perfect.

To Martha, he was anything but. And seeing him again yesterday in his arena, identifying the damage beneath his rough beauty, only confirmed that.

Between the hours of two and seven, Martha's party of four had been reduced by half, but she hadn't minded that the others had slipped away. She'd woken up where she'd fallen asleep, deep in the suppleness of a club chair, and had been relieved that someone had turned off the plasma-screen television and made at least a half-assed effort to clear away their mess. What she *hadn't* wanted to see was an image of blood and gore—already her dreams had been spooked, thanks to the Ouija board she'd discovered in storage, too much liquor and old horror movies of the *Nightmare on Elm Street* and *The Texas Chainsaw Massacre* variety.

But she'd prefer even that to the look of untainted rage on her mother's face. Tem had burst through Martha's doors unannounced, and, from the looks of the high-end retailers' bags she'd set down at her feet, had been raring to start decorating Martha's place for Christmas. Now she looked as though she'd rather do more damage than Freddy Krueger's most depraved fantasies could conjure.

Better get you on your way, Gideon. In college, Gideon, then an aspiring model and crappy barista, had earned his stripes as a friend—the strong shoulder to cry away her frustrations on, the guy who called her on her crap when she deserved it and stayed out of her way when she needed space. They'd had sex once, while skinny-dipping during a group getaway in Nantucket last summer. And when Martha had told him that it wouldn't happen again, he'd accepted it.

The very least she could do now was make sure he returned to Los Angeles in one piece and lived long enough to see his big-deal national cologne commercial premiere.

Martha sat up, trying for nonchalance. Not fear—never that. Her oldest sister had once joked that their parents fed off fear, but Martha secretly wondered just how much truth lay buried in the barb.

Tem's designer high heels stabbed the floor as she approached Martha and her friend. "Martha Chastity Blue—"

A male snort had daughter and mother snapping their attention to Gideon.

"Your middle name's *Chastity*?" Another snort of laughter.

Before Martha could warn him to shut the hell up, her mother intervened. "Yes, that's her middle name. Her father and I didn't foresee the irony."

That stung. A lot. Martha cast her gaze downward, to her poinsettia-red toenails. She'd get up and walk, and the dig wouldn't hurt anymore. "C'mon, guy." Unfolding herself from the sofa, she entwined her arm with his and steered him toward the kitchen, gracing her mother with a neutral glance as they passed. "I'll pour you a cup of joe."

Once they cleared the threshold, she dropped his arm. "Done laughing?"

"Sorry." He pressed his palms together and bowed his head. "Were you serious about that coffee, 'cause…"

Martha's incredulous glare had him trailing off and scanning the granite countertops for any contraption that might provide his morning caffeine fix. "It's fine," she said after a moment. Taking pity—after all, what fault was it of his that he had the Y chromosome and was incapable of understanding a woman's emotional plumbing?—she grabbed a mug from the tree on the island and filled it halfway with hazelnut-flavored salvation. "I suppose Chastity *is* ironic. The only name that would be more ironic is Virgin." She tried to smile, make light of her mother's words, but a snap of embarrassment killed the effort.

"She hurt your feelings." Gideon set down his mug. "Tell her that."

"No. Get going." She punched his arm, without any genuine force behind the gesture. "Don't want you to be a casualty of the Tempest."

Gideon took a final gulp of coffee, then left Martha alone with her mother.

"You spent the night with a man who didn't even know your middle name?" Tem inquired, gliding into the kitchen, picking up the attack where it had left off. "What's his name, by the way?"

"Gideon Crane."

Tem eyed the room with transparent distaste. "Your sister never used this space to its potential, but at least it was always clean. Am I seeing three empty bourbon bottles?"

"Bourbon ice cream requires bourbon."

"Based on the fact that the liquor bottles outnumber the ice cream containers three to one, I'd say your recipe was heavier on the bourbon."

Not exactly. When we ran out of ice cream, we drank straight bourbon while trying to make contact with the otherworld using a Ouija board. The retort was sliding around on Martha's tongue, but she kept her mouth shut as she carried her friend's mug to the sink.

"Is that hazelnut coffee in the brewer?" Tem inquired. "I'd like a cup."

"Got plenty of clean mugs on the tree." After a beat of silence, Martha turned away from the sink to find her mother ogling the array of mismatched mugs with a narrow-eyed, twisted-mouth expression. "Problem, Ma?"

"The Pillivuyt porcelain mugs I bought when you moved out of the Bellagio. Where are they?"

"Put away." *Be patient. She's your mother. She gave you life a full ten years after she thought she was done with breastfeeding and potty training.* "Why don't I fetch one?"

"Quickly." Tem cast a subtle glance at her wristwatch. "Then get yourself dressed."

Martha scanned the chef-style room. As gorgeous as the custom-made white cabinetry, stainless steel appliances and abundant windows were, the kitchen could be blinding when sunlight hit it just right. And the immediate problem was that the cabinets rose high up the walls, practically kissing the coffered ceiling.

Of course, the mug her mother wanted was one Martha had given a home on the highest shelf.

Easing her bum onto the counter, she gave a little gasp at the granite's chilled temperature on her skin. Undeterred, she carefully got to her knees.

"What the hell, Martha?" Tem whispered, frozen on the safety of a modest stool at the island counter. "I didn't tell you to climb—"

"Climbing's good exercise."

"Prancing around on a countertop is an ER visit in the making." Tem's footsteps sounded on the floor. "These cabinets are tall, which is why Danica kept a stepladder handy."

"Danica doesn't have a pair of stems like mine." Martha rose up on her tiptoes, reaching.

"Be careful— Oh, God, my eyes!"

"What?"

"The knickers you're wearing belong in a sex shop."

"Or a lingerie convention, which is where I bought them. Got a visual on the mugs."

"About your gentleman. Crane. Is it serious?"

Martha pivoted to face her mother. "If you call plans to get hitched and name our firstborn child Ichabod *serious*, then yes."

"Want the kid gloves off? We can do it that way. I'm

done forcing myself to be polite. You're the one who was caught with a strange man in her house."

"Gideon's not strange, and he isn't the only person who spent the night. My friend Leigh Bridges stayed, as well. Get the Post-it off that bourbon bottle on the end of the row there."

Tem touched a finger to each of her dainty pearl tear-drop earrings. Always so elegant, so regal, in designer fashions and a flattering hairstyle that made her appear refined rather than distinctly middle-aged, she was nothing short of classic beauty perfected. A "style icon," a fashion critic at the BET Awards had declared her.

That had been a few years ago—before Martha's sister Danica's divorce from a music mogul, before the Blue family had immersed itself in professional sports—but the assessment still held true. Tem's ability to remain timelessly lovely through the strains of beauty pageantry, the stress of bringing up three daughters and the pressure of acquiring and cultivating an NFL team was a marvelous mystery.

"What happened here last night?" Tem asked, ignoring the bottles altogether.

"If you won't read the note for yourself, I'll recite it verbatim. 'Bart has an early morning. We're taking off. FYI, a Ouija and horror flick cocktail is terrifying. Let's do it again soon. Kisses.'"

"Who's Bart?"

"Leigh's boyfriend."

"Then you were hosting an orgy?"

"I'm not turning this house into a sex dungeon." Martha returned to her task, retrieving one of the basket-weave mugs.

Tem sighed, and it sounded almost anxious. "Speaking of your butt, please get some real clothes on. An NFL team publicist should care that people might see her indecent." Another sigh, though this one was heavy with weariness. "Quit shutting your eyes and ears to the truth. Everything counts. Your reputation counts. It counts, Martha, whether or not a young woman must depend on a spreadsheet to keep track of the men she's had sex with."

Martha was relieved to have her face half buried in shelves and dishes. She wiggled her nose to ease the prickly forewarning of tears. "A spreadsheet. Is that what you recommend? Maybe there's a phone app for that."

Tem's voice was softer, perhaps with regret, as she said, "What you do today, the people you let get close to you today, affects your tomorrow. That's all I'm saying."

"But it's *my* today. It's *my* tomorrow. This is my kitchen now, and if I choose not to use a stepladder to reach a high shelf, then damn it, that's my choice."

"Um—"

"And if I want to turn this house into the nastiest, most hard-core sex dungeon Las Vegas has ever seen, then that's my choice, too."

As though the room had been trapped in a choke hold, the oxygen seemed to vanish. There were no sounds except for the rush of Martha's pulse in her ears. The atmosphere had changed.

Turning her back to the cabinets, she saw Tem in her French fashion-doll getup with her gaze averted. No, not simply averted, but pinned on Joaquin Ryder.

The man whose hard, angry sexiness ate up the air in the room. The man whose vicious rejection had once sank into her as savagely as attraction did now.

The man whose coal-black stare—she knew with untainted certainty—had been fixed on Martha's ass.

Chapter 3

A gentleman, Joaquin was not. Anyone who'd ever held the misguided impression that he was, didn't make the mistake twice. Confronted with a worm's-eye view of Martha's rump peeking out of striped bikini panties, a gentleman would've shifted his attention to something that didn't spike his heart rate. A decent man wouldn't have swallowed the image of her stretching up toward a high shelf.

A man who wasn't hunting for trouble would've interrupted his body's primal response to what he'd overheard.

If I want to turn this house into the nastiest, most hardcore sex dungeon Las Vegas has ever seen, then that's my choice, too.

Whatever argument he'd walked in on, it had Temperance Blue on the losing end. Belatedly he remembered that Tem stood within slapping distance of him. He sent a shallow prayer that cooling his thoughts would ease the hardness in his crotch. As Martha turned to face them, he pulled his gaze from her nicely displayed butt cheeks to the diamond ring that circled one of her toes.

Damn. Even her feet were beautiful.

Too slow to detect the danger of standing in her house, of reinserting himself into her life to help Marshall and Tem while assuaging his own guilt, Joaquin realized he was against the ropes again.

He didn't like that—to be pushed to desperation. Part of the glory of fighting was that every risk he took was on *his* terms.

"Charming, Martha," Tem said.

"I wasn't expecting a first-thing-in-the-morning ambush." Martha pointed down at Joaquin with a pearly-white mug. "Catch." When he cupped his hands, she scoffed. "Sharp, broken things and I don't get along. And I'm not taking a chance on dropping the mug I flashed my derriere to get from this cabinet. I meant catch *me*."

Joaquin's brain stayed stuck on *flashed my derriere* until she said, "You're tall, strong and in my way for a reason, aren't you?" Softly arched brows rose a millimeter over obsidian eyes.

Not giving her the satisfaction of his agitation, he held out his arms. She jumped without hesitation, landing securely in his grip with a whisper of a sigh. Privately he relished the vanilla scent on her hair, the gentle sleep-puffiness of her eyelids, the jiggle of her breasts, and her subtle curves and angles.

In the span of seven heartbeats, she was twisting out of his arms. Unfortunately, he'd cradled her a moment too long—because now he suspected that she was the sexiest thing he would ever see or hold. And he didn't have a single defense.

"Coffee's in the brewer over there," Martha said to a stunned-speechless Tem, relinquishing the mug. "I'll walk Joaquin out."

"But—but I invited him here to visit you," Tem protested. "As a surprise."

"The drawback to surprises is that there's no guarantee they'll pan out. I've got a date with a six-jet shower. After that I'm going to the stadium."

"Martha, I thought you were taking a personal day to decorate this house for the holidays. It's almost Christmas and there's nothing festive on the property."

"I was going to take a personal day to listen to you dictate how I should decorate this house. Now I'd rather reacquaint Joaquin with the door and then apply my energy to PR business." Martha brushed past him, making tracks for the foyer.

"Vegas is smaller than it seems," she said to him once he jogged down the rough stone steps and joined her in the semi-privacy of the hushed lawn. The security gate was open the way he'd found it when he had eased his Cadillac Escalade past the stream and rocks bordering the driveway. Sunlight played over her form and washed the rustling, shaggy grounds. "Our paths are bound to cross again."

"Not if you don't want them to." He had visited Nevada on a handful of occasions over the past four years, to either fight or promote a fight, and had managed to slip out of the state without encountering her.

Screw the fallout—he'd do the same thing now if it meant sparing her more hurt.

"I'll keep my head down, win the match I came here to win, and leave. I don't want to hurt you again."

Martha stared in contemplation. Then she laughed. The ring of it forced him off his axis. "Your life is about hurting people, Joaquin. You're America's number one boxer because you make fighting look like art. Causing pain, destroying people—you've perfected it. Knowing who you are—what you are—makes me immune to you."

There wasn't a trace of the fragile sincerity he'd witnessed in the gym yesterday. Coldness stood in its place.

Behind the wheel of his truck, he captured a final glimpse of her as she, with her arctic attitude, taut legs, flimsy sweater and satisfied-with-herself smirk, spun and retreated into the house.

I don't know what game we're playing, Martha. But I don't lose. I never lose.

At half past seven, Martha turned off the Tiffany lamp on her mirrored office desk. Darkness collapsed onto the room. Light from the outer hall bled into the shadows, and she could hear a drone of voices. Corporate reorganization had recently combined public relations personnel with the advertising and marketing departments, forcing them to coexist on the admin building's fourth floor—called "Schmoozers' World," or more informally, "S-Dubs." Most of the Las Vegas Slayers' front office schmoozers had probably just poured the last drops of stale caffeine from carafes to cups in order to stave off fatigue and finish tasks, meet deadlines and connect with overseas contacts far into the night.

Martha had immersed herself in team promotions and publicity. The only reprieve she'd allowed herself was the elegant midafternoon luncheon in the conference room. Marshall and Tem had permitted her to join the business operations meeting providing she refrained from chiming in.

The logic behind the stipulation—she had a knack for talking her way into and out of trouble and she was a fresh college graduate who'd majored in communication studies but unofficially minored in mischief—hadn't dampened her enthusiasm for the opportunity to watch the franchise's biggest players in their element.

Neither Marshall nor Tem grasped that her hunger to strengthen their legacy was so genuine that she'd passed the GMAT and was a part-time Lee Business School student. Enrolling in the graduate program had been liberating, even though it remained a secret. She wasn't ready to lay her ambitions at her parents'—her employers'—feet, only to have those ambitions punctured with discouragement.

What she *was* ready for involved vodka and a dance floor. She grabbed her tablet, a pile of crisp folders and her purse. Her friend Leigh had texted earlier to beg off their plans: RAIN CHECK ON FOUNDATION ROOM. GOING TO D.C. WITH DAD TONIGHT. NEXT MARTINIS ON ME!

That hadn't come as a surprise, since Leigh, whom she'd met only months ago at a wedding, was steadfastly following in her CNN correspondent father's footsteps.

Martha stepped into hall traffic, counterflowing a barrage of suit-and-tie advertising execs, half of whom paused to admire her walk-away. She was less concerned with their perusal than she was interested in finding someone with whom to share a round of drinks. A social drinker, she preferred conversation with her alcohol. She stopped at her friend's cubicle, taking a moment to admire the small fiber-optic tree on the desktop. "Can I interest you in martinis at the Foundation Room?"

"Yes!" Chelle Vine pushed away from her computer, but didn't seem excited as she began revolving in her chair. "Too bad I can't, though. Late night with my cubicle mates. With a few more Red Bulls and a crapload of luck, we'll finalize the tweaks to the team party before sunup. Our entertainment headliner fell through. He's apparently shooting a few scenes for a film, and there's a conflict. But our second choice was waiting in the wings."

"Thank God for second choices." But Martha fumed. DZ Haze, an ex-convict who'd preached in lockup and rapped once he was released, was at the pinnacle of hip-hop superstardom. She'd treated his publicist and the record label's top execs to VIP Las Vegas experiences just to book the artist. It had been a personal triumph because she'd succeeded without the aid of the man who *always* got asses to move in the music industry: Marion Reeves, her sister's ex-husband. Now she felt used, offended and even more determined to get her way.

If her parents got wind of the performer's disrespect, of her failure to keep him committed, she'd appear weak.

In a world of overblown egos, multimillion-dollar deals and cutthroat business maneuvers, weakness wasn't flattering.

"Not official yet," she said to Chelle, "but I'm getting DZ Haze back on the schedule. A headliner needs a solid opener to get everyone hyped. That's what we'll tell our backup. Keep it confidential."

Chelle's chair abruptly stopped spinning. How the woman managed to remain sitting upright without spilling onto the floor, dizzy, Martha couldn't explain. "Evening, Mrs. Blue," Chelle said.

Martha noticed the boost in the distinct sounds of productivity—people shuffling papers, tapping keyboards, slapping staplers—and would've smiled had she not suspected that she, rather than on-the-clock slackers, was the reason for Tem's voyage to S-Dubs.

"A word before you head out, Martha?" Tem asked.

"Absolutely." To Chelle she said, "I'll have a Madagascar margarita in your honor."

"Order it extra spicy."

"No. I value my taste buds." Chuckling, she wagged her index finger in farewell and began walking alongside Tem.

"We'll take the owners' elevator down," her mother informed her, strutting with purpose. In a few strides Martha had fallen behind her.

The owners' elevator contained a pair of tufted chairs and a stoic-faced attendant who resembled an action-movie Secret Service agent.

Though Tem settled into one of the chairs, Martha didn't follow suit. She failed to see the point when their destination was the main floor.

No expense had been spared to renovate the building's lobby. It gleamed and twinkled, and was nearly as overwhelmingly grand as Martha's favorite New York City relaxation spot, Hôtel Plaza Athénée.

Passing the concierge's marble-topped desk, Tem led her to a settee near the soaring Christmas tree. The professionals hired to decorate the stadium for the holidays had achieved a blissful marriage of creativity and class, but Martha was partial to the extravagant hand-painted glass ornaments that displayed this season's Slayers' names and jersey numbers.

"I'm organizing a formal family dinner, since your sister Danica chose to twist the knife of embarrassment and not share Thanksgiving with the family—"

"Ma, it wasn't like that," Martha interrupted. All right, maybe it was a little unflattering that the team's freshly re-signed GM had indulged in a Thanksgiving getaway with the team's freshly reinstated quarterback. But her sister and Dex hadn't asked to fall in love. They had made themselves suffer to ignore it for the sake of obligations. Now that they'd found the kind of connection that others lived and died without knowing, shouldn't that be what mattered? "Dex is part of Danica's family. She lives with him, sleeps with him, and she wanted to spend Thanksgiving with him."

"Oregon, though? An orchard?"

Martha shrugged. "It's where Dex grew up, and it's spectacular. If you make an effort to visit them instead of popping up in my neck of the woods, you could see the photographs yourself." After several seconds of Tem's narrow-eyed glare, Martha hastened to add, "I know you miss her."

"I miss having her as part of the team. Marshall does, too. We brought Charlotte to the training staff for her potential and persistence. We hired you to give you guidance and stability. But Danica…we wanted her here at our side, as our GM."

"Well, Ma, she wants to work at Faith House and have a future with Dex." Faith House was the nonprofit teen out-reach shelter Danica had founded. In exchange for owner-ship of her sister's former house, Martha had agreed to volunteer at the shelter. "She has a good life now. Char-lotte's got a good life, too, with Nate."

"Nate Franco. Dex Harper. With *my* girls." Tem sounded weary.

"Okay, they're not altar boys. But, *come on, Ma*, the Blue family Christmas card photo's a lot sexier this year."

Major understatement, but to press the issue would only reveal Martha's own kink for badass men.

Martha didn't date. She'd never had a boyfriend. She had lovers and friends. And wasn't that her prerogative?

Wasn't it her choice to never have sex with the same man twice?

So far she'd managed to keep the details of her sexcapades to herself, which wasn't easy when something as benign as laughing with a man could be misconstrued as cause for internet shaming.

"You didn't bring anyone to the family Christmas card photo shoot," Tem commented loftily.

Because to do that would've implied that she was committed to someone, which she never had been and never would be. "I haven't met anyone who's Christmas card worthy."

"Just consider this. When you come home tonight you'll see that it's remarkably tidier than it was when you left. I paid my household staff to clean it. They don't judge—but I will, because I'm your mother."

"Judge away, Ma." Martha turned toward the tree, bracing herself. Two Tem lectures in one day? Did she—anyone—deserve this?

"A responsible home owner with the financial blessings you have should secure her own housekeeping. Or she should paint the town less and clean the house more. Seems every other night you go off the grid, Martha, and neither your father nor I can reach you. Where do you go?"

University of Nevada, Las Vegas. The library. Places where I feel good about myself and my future, where I can accomplish goals you think are out of my league. "You already answered that question," she said. "I paint the town." For now, at least, lying was the best way to safeguard her pride.

"Slow down, Martha."

"Slow down? Why—so some man can catch up to me? No, thank you."

"Then make time for your family. That includes Joaquin. I was livid watching you all but run him out of the house this morning."

"Want me to apologize?"

"Next time he sacrifices his own priorities to visit you, be a respectful hostess to your guest."

"Which is he, Ma? Family or guest? Or just an acquaintance who hasn't exactly made time for the Blues in recent years?"

"Joaquin's career should come first. I realize you looked up to him as an older brother of sorts, but he's not your brother. You shouldn't feel entitled to priority in his life. He can't care about you as much as you might think he should."

Didn't she already know? Hadn't she had four years to tattoo the message into her mind? "Don't worry, Ma." She stepped away from the Christmas tree and the conversation. "I know exactly how little I matter to Joaquin Ryder."

A camera flashed as Martha stepped out of the Blues' private tinted-window BMW in front of Mandalay Bay. "You're more of a celebrity in this city than you think," the driver commented, shutting her door.

"Or that pair of paparazzi was tired of stalking this place for real celebs and photographed the first person who popped out of a car with dark windows," she retorted with a grin.

As she cut a path to the entrance in her baggy Christmas-spirit-red sweater, destroyed skinny jeans and stilettos, she sensed someone watching her. Peeking to her left, she found a heavily bearded man in a puffy jacket and stained pants.

"Want a picture, or what?"

The man looked to his companion, who seemed startled that she'd stopped to speak. "Yeah. And can we ask you about Joaquin Ryder? Common knowledge says he's close to the Blue family."

"What about him?"

"We got a tip that he'd be showing up here tonight. We want to ask him about fight night."

Martha hadn't gotten that tip. She scanned the face of the towering Mandalay Bay. If she was going to convince Joaquin that she'd shrugged off the past, she had to prove that he had zero effect on her decisions. She'd left Slayers Stadium, showered off the workday and come out to simply dance at the Foundation Room. There was no choice *but* to follow through.

"Can't help you there," she told the paparazzi.

"The picture?" Puffy Jacket reminded her.

Martha smiled kindly. "Of course. In fact, give your pal the camera. C'mon over and say cheese." Once the camera clicked, she went inside. The paparazzi population hadn't been overly pleasant to her, broadcasting her mistakes and finding scandal where there was none, but Puffy Jacket and his friend had given her valuable information.

Joaquin was going to be here tonight—if he hadn't already slipped inside undetected. All Martha had to do was pretend she didn't give a crap.

In the exclusive Foundation Room, her favorite bartender gave her a sweet martini that she nursed while standing and swaying to the music. Though members-only, the space was filling fast with patrons all hard-up for drinks, laughs and dancing.

Giving herself up to the music, she gyrated to the center of the crowd. So high over the Las Vegas Strip with the bass shaking her bones, she didn't know a more thrilling sensation.

"Moves like those were made for bedrooms and poles."

Martha startled, forgetting that she wasn't supposed to care about the past or that Joaquin in the present posed a much bigger threat to her defenses. It wasn't supposed to influence her one way or the other that he was stone, inside and out, and his seriousness was so deep that frown creases bracketed his firm mouth. Time and again, it compelled her to tell him a knock-knock joke to lure a smile.

His single-dimpled smile alone was a glorious thing. In combination with his shaved-to-the-scalp hair, dark eyes and tasty-as-brown-sugar complexion, his image had supplied her with many nights' worth of red-letter dreams.

The bastard. In the end, that's what he'd wanted her to walk away believing he was.

So why was he in her way—again?

"I don't dance for opinions. I dance for myself," Martha told him, turning on the congested dance floor to behold him in a suit that was on the brink of shoving her into a spontaneous orgasm. "This is kind of my hangout, Joaquin."

"All members are welcome."

"Well, Las Vegas is clearly running out of hot spots if a place can appeal to a man with your tastes and a woman with mine. We're very different people."

"Can we talk—off the dance floor?"

"That might be a problem, seeing as I came here to dance." Yeah, she was being mulish, petulant and difficult, but he'd treated her in practically the same regard yesterday at his uncle's gym.

And she *had* come here to dance.

Joaquin's mouth hovered at her ear. "Please, Martha."

Attraction was a living, breathing thing between them. Could fate truly be so unfair that he was completely closed off to the lust that rattled her as thoroughly as the music's bass?

"I'm making my way to the bar for a Madagascar margarita." Dancing to the bar, she felt him follow her. He sat on a stool, waiting as she ordered the drink then took a brave swallow.

The liquid damn near sizzled all the way down, doing

nothing to calm her high-octane horniness. Heat on top of heat only made things hotter...

"Change your mind about the talking, Joaquin?"

"Yesterday, at the gym, I acted like a jerk."

"Uh...I know that." Martha pushed the margarita across the bar, then, still rocking to the music's heavy rhythm, positioned herself in front of him. "I was there."

"I'm trying to tell you I'm sorry, Martha."

Fingers of light and shadow streaked over them as he spoke the words. "What?"

Joaquin's hands shot forward to clasp her hips and urge her closer. Martha braced her palms on his thighs, felt the heat of his tight muscles beneath the fabric of his pants. Yesterday, in training mode, he'd appeared menacing. Tonight, cleaned up in a suit, he was dangerous.

Teasing danger, Martha sank her fingers into his solid flesh. Added more force to her writhing. Eliminated all the distance as she edged farther between his thighs. "Not sure if I heard you right," she murmured onto his jaw...a resilient, angular jaw that had withstood so many harsh strikes. All she wanted was to lay her lips there.

No women in his entourage, no willing body that he'd taken for pleasure, could give him the compassion she could with a kiss. She hadn't planned to end up this invincible fighter's weakness. But, since he wanted no weaknesses, he didn't want Martha.

Yet here they were in spite of even that.

Countering, "You heard me," he let his hands trail her denim. The rough pads of his fingers scraped her skin through the haphazard tears in her destroyed jeans. "Martha..."

"Want me to stop, Joaquin? Am I easier to handle standing still?"

Rock. Grind. Sway. Keep dancing.

Need and resistance clashed in his irises. "I—"

Not another rejection—and for damn sure not from this

man. Moving against him slowly now, she cut off his words, robbing him of the chance to test how effortlessly he could reopen her invisible wounds. "Get off my territory."

"Martha." A strong finger curled into a rip high on her hip, and his groan was so deep and intimate, she felt as though *she'd* made the guttural sound. "I didn't ask you to stop."

Chapter 4

"But," Martha said softly, the margarita-scented word grazing his lips, "if I wanted to, I could stop."

The woman was practically in his lap, shackling him to his bar stool with lust.

Joaquin's first mistake tonight had been to touch her. Dipping his finger into that tear in her jeans. Raking her skin. It had been a purely idiotic thing to do when just the picture of her dancing in the crush had kicked his body into low vibration. If he'd known ahead of time that she'd be here…he might've shown up sooner.

Joaquin killed the thought. It had been trying enough to battle his instincts to clear the Foundation Room and finish what Martha had begun. Groaning—letting that control slither through his grasp—had been his second mistake.

He couldn't allow another. Mistakes indicated disorder. Disorder was interference. Training for the most hyped-up main-card fight of his career, he needed to dodge or defeat interference.

Dodge Martha, though? Not likely. Only hours ago she'd warned him of what he'd found to be true when he'd stepped into this room: Las Vegas didn't harbor enough hiding places. Not for two people who *should* want to avoid each other, but for whatever reason didn't. Stacked on top of that was what he'd told Marshall Blue in the ring at Jules's gym.

I'll keep her close. She won't jeopardize your business on my watch. That's a promise.

Sealed with a grave nod, Joaquin had given his word that he'd deliver. Before he'd fought his way to money and celebrity, the only thing of value he had was his word. A promise from him was a rare thing, but his promises were never offered lightly and were always—*always*—honored.

Martha's nails dug deeper into his thighs.

Control kept him silent, but the impulse to manipulate that rip in her jeans until he could fit his entire hand inside had him brutally clenching his teeth. If he couldn't dodge her, then the singular option was to defeat whatever effects she—and her soft hair, luscious frown and trouble-hungry hands—had on him.

"A camera-phone click, and anyone can paint a picture of you giving me a lap dance at Mandalay Bay." Even with a demanding hard-on, he could still be pragmatic. "Does that concern you?"

"Does it concern you that a picture could be painted of you getting a lap dance at Mandalay Bay?" was her casual response. "No, right, because you'd be seen as a man just having a good time. Centuries of struggles, so much social progress, and still a man's free to celebrate his sexuality when a woman has to downplay hers."

"Unfair. I didn't say it wasn't." The genuine apprehension in her expression pricked his resolve, dug in where he was defenseless. "Switch places, then, and I'll give you a lap dance."

The lights shimmied over her as she rolled her eyes. "Funny, Joaquin. But I like you where you are." She jerked her body all nice and tight up against him. "Some other things I like? Flirting. Sex. Getting off. I'm turned on right now—so wet right now—"

"This is you downplaying your sexuality?" *Bold* didn't begin to describe her approach. In public, she was telling him things only a lover should hear…sharing secrets meant for a man who at least deserved her.

He wasn't that man.

"These are facts. Another fact—I can let you go."

"Then stop, if that's what you want to do, Martha."

"Or..." Her focus drifted down to his lap as her fingers relaxed. "I could come a little closer." She pushed her hips forward, and damn him, he was urging her, deeply stroking her flesh through tattered denim. "And do this."

Joaquin didn't want to give her that, the satisfaction of knowing she could reach him on some level—any level. Yet he let his gaze trip over the image of her thumbs settling on either side of the hard ridge in his pants. She firmly pressed down, moving her thumbs back and forth, further tightening the fabric that his erection was straining beneath.

"I *could*, Joaquin," she whispered, "tease you like this until you money-shot in these nice designer pants. Then I could tear you down and demand that you—and I'll say it again—*get off my territory*."

Damn it. He was apologizing for yesterday, but all this catch-and-release teasing, all the pain she was trying to hide, was about what had happened four years ago. That one damaging night. "Screwing with men's minds—you've gotten good at it. Too good."

Indifferent, she reached over his shoulder for her margarita. "You're too serious."

Intercepting her, he wrapped his fingers around her wrist, felt her pulse pound. "Who're you here with?" When she mumbled something about being on her own time tonight, he pressed, "Drive yourself?"

"A BMW and a driver are on call."

"Get your phone, take him off call. You and I need to go back to that place."

"Where's 'that place'?"

"The gym. It's another cold December night. Key's in my pocket."

"So the stage is set for a do-over?" A mocking snort followed. "That's bewilderingly romantic—for you, anyway."

"It's not about being romantic." He rubbed his thumb

over her wrist where her pulse continued to leap quickly, resisting the pressure of his touch. "It's about taking every measure to get you past what happened."

"And at the same time get you past your guilt?" Martha shrugged as though she didn't care, and had the quick beat dancing against his thumb not betrayed her, he might've believed it. "Don't judge me for holding on, when you're holding on, too."

The dig rendered him mute, as he uncurled his fingers from her wrist, dropped cash onto the bar and carved a path for her through the blockade of elite guests swallowing liquor and writhing in sync with the music.

Martha belonged here, nestled in high-stakes, top-floor Las Vegas luxury. He belonged where they were headed next—a street-level gym that was more acquainted with graffiti and games of street craps than with priceless furnishings and imported champagne. Wealth, glory, international fame—none of it had rezoned his territory. None of it had changed him.

"Paparazzi were patrolling out front," Martha said, her voice just behind him. "Anyone in a puffy jacket accost you?"

"No. I have ways of making myself invisible to folks in puffy jackets who want to accost me."

"Can't say the same. I posed for a picture with the guy. It seemed to pacify him."

"Engineer a network that operates on trust, and situations like that'll be easier to control," he advised. "You're in my network, from now until I leave you tucked in safe at your house."

"Hey." Martha came around in front of him. "That alpha put-helpless-Martha-under-a-man's-protection bullshit? Save it. I may not fight for a living and step in the middle of violence every day, but I'm capable of protecting myself."

Having fought professionally for over a decade, he'd encountered plenty of female boxers and mixed martial artists and knew to never underestimate a woman's physical strength and mental strategy. With her temper, unpredictable nature and the pride she took in self-defense, Martha had the tools to neutralize an aggressor.

Those incredible legs could probably kick a man's balls up to his throat.

He admired her like hell for that. But when he offered his protection, he expected it to be accepted—with gratitude, not offense. "Damn straight, you can defend yourself. You just won't need to when you're with me."

"Joaquin—"

"Thank me in the truck," he cut her off, wrangling control of the conversation. "Let's move, if you want to bypass another run-in with paparazzi."

Swallowing whatever protest waited on her tongue, Martha shadowed him.

They were going to his uncle's gym to retrace steps and reopen wounds—and there wouldn't be anything pleasurable about it.

Finally, they reached Sig, the ex-military Las Vegas security specialist Joaquin kept on retainer to manage the "street" eyes and ears responsible for eliminating any potential obstacles—from face-to-face altercations to unwanted photos—that might complicate his casual walk from the building to his ride.

Sig had ensured that the same valet who'd parked Joaquin's Escalade had it revved and waiting a half block from Mandalay Bay's rear exit. Recruiting only the best security in Nevada and Florida, and keeping them loyal on his payroll, was no modest expense. But the cost was unimportant when it could deter the hellhounds his ex-fiancée had sicced on him after their last courtroom battle. Especially when it afforded him the brief moments of privacy and anonymity he stole as he walked into the glimmering night with Martha.

Never had they had this—space and time together for

something as simple as walking side by side, as adults. Equals. The differences in their ages and upbringing had from the get-go placed her out of his realm. Investing and professional boxing had monopolized his attention so completely that he hadn't noticed Martha's slow and steady evolution from an indulgent little girl in need of a knight, to a stunner of a woman who could fight for herself.

Inside the Escalade, Martha tugged her seat belt into place and swiveled against the cradling leather to face him as the truck joined the flow of traffic. "No Tor and Othello hanging about?"

"Why are you saying their names in *my* truck?"

Martha's amused grin was impossible to disregard. "If the challenge is to talk about you, and only you, while in this vehicle, then I'm extremely prepared to accept."

"Meaning?"

"All right. Play it dense. *Meaning*, Joaquin, that I'd be happy to tell you about yourself. For starters, you're acting like a jerk again." She tsked. "In this case, it's a clear symptom of jealousy."

Jealousy? Her question had been perfectly innocuous, one deserving of a response that wasn't saturated with... yeah, jealousy. Shit. It was his dysfunction that he got hot under the collar at the thought of her laying her affections at the feet of any man who wasn't him. Jealousy, he concluded, was ruthless. If he was going to open himself up to that kind of distraction, he ought to accept defeat now and not even step into the ring at MGM Grand.

"I went out tonight to assess my surroundings, which is a process I prefer to do alone. Getting a feel for the city helps me prepare for a fight."

"You grew up in Vegas. Shouldn't every square inch of this city be imprinted on your brain?"

"Cities are fluid. They change. And I haven't lived here for four years."

"Oh. Guess I can appreciate that—how something

you've known all your life can become unfamiliar. How someone you know so well can turn into a stranger."

Save the blame and the finger-pointing for the gym, Martha.

Promptly twisting to sit straight ahead, as though she'd caught his unspoken words, she commented, "This truck suits you. The sound of the engine's part growl, part purr, as if warning of a hidden energy—maybe anxiety—beneath all the cool. It's powerful but at the same time sleek. It's a beast and can claim the road if it wanted to. But it has to be controlled."

"Contained?"

"Cared for."

God. Damn. Yet again she perplexed him. It wasn't the sugary sweetness of her fragrance, or the spice in her voice. It was her sincerity—a sharp dagger aimed right at a fissure in his armor. "Been making assessments of your own?" he remarked, signaling a turn and sparing her a look. "I am a beast—a machine. Machines aren't cared for. They're conditioned for optimum performance."

"And if the machine doesn't reach this elusive *optimum performance*?"

"If it fails to achieve its purpose? Then it's junkyard scrap."

"Still basing your identity on how many championships you rack up, I take it." There was no pitying tsk tacked on, no note of derision in her voice, but her retort was a judgment. "About the paparazzi at the hotel? They were sniffing around for you. Fight-night fever's infecting everyone."

"Including you?" Why he hadn't resolved to just drive in complete quiet, he didn't know. The solemn question was already out there, floating between them, pining for an answer.

"I probably won't catch the main card. My idea of exciting entertainment doesn't involve watching you risk your life in a boxing ring. And the play-offs have my attention.

My family's after a championship of our own. You're not the only one with titles to win and purposes to achieve." Done pretending that she was paying attention to the crowds and lights and downtown roads, Martha swung her body around toward him again. "Peppermint candy canes!"

Joaquin stifled a groan. What kind of hell would she give him for keeping Brach's in his truck's cup holder? "It's Christmastime. And I like candy canes," he defended in a dead-serious tone. "Give me one? Taking off that plastic is a two-handed job, and I need one on the wheel."

"Ah. Ah. Ah," she teased, grabbing the pair of canes. "You've *got* to be more resourceful than that."

Braking to a stop behind a row of vehicles halted at a red light, he signaled for the candy and froze with his hand in midair when she lifted a cane to her lips.

The leather sighed under her weight as she shifted farther. "You have to use your teeth." Leaning close, she flicked the tip of her tongue against the end of the cane. "Bite."

Joaquin's hand felt welded onto the steering wheel, he clutched it so tightly.

Martha efficiently stripped the plastic wrapper from the candy cane. Once it was bare, she motioned for him to open his mouth.

Clamping his teeth onto the hook, he was about to turn forward when she stilled him with her hands on his cheeks. Then she bobbed, bit down and snapped off half of the stick.

"Green light." Martha retreated to her seat, holding her piece between thumb and forefinger as her tongue stroked the jagged end. A chorus of blaring horns underscored her words.

Apparently, Joaquin was supposed to drag his foot off the brake and drive, and deny that what she was doing to a piece of candy had his erection bowing up again. He sent her a glare. Anything to knock off the edge. "Why take half of mine when you have one of your own?"

"Saving it for later." As if suspicious he might steal it back, she dropped the wrapped candy cane into her handbag.

"I wouldn't have let your sly ass into my truck if I'd figured you'd pilfer my Brach's stash."

"A grown man should learn the virtues of sharing PDQ." Martha was all but laughing as she chomped down on the cane. "Besides, you love my sly ass."

"*Love* isn't in my vocabulary." A woman could say she loved her boyfriend and in the same breath say she loved a pair of Italian high heels. A different woman could swear to love her fiancé, only to hours later be caught screwing someone else in his house. Another woman could starve her son of love and teach him that all that mattered was fighting for survival.

Silence dropped, settled, thickened. Martha had no response. Good. Maybe she'd let the issue pass. It wasn't until Joaquin had swung the truck into the parking lot of Ryder's Boxing Club, jerked the key in the ignition and watched darkness fill the interior that he realized he'd lowered the gloves too soon and she was simply awaiting the opportunity to strike.

"Offended by four-letter words?" she said, carving into that blessed silence as she alighted from the truck. "You have no problem using other four-letter words in the ring."

Joaquin rounded the vehicle, stopping in a spread-legged stance in front of where she stood beside the ajar passenger door. "So you've been watching me fight."

Flustered, she stammered, bumping the door shut with her hip. "Uh—not—well, not habitually. Folks beating the hell out of each other and calling it a sport? Thanks, but it's not for me." Recovered now, she evaded him on her booty-swinging walk to the gym's entrance.

"It wasn't always for me, either," he admitted, joining

her on the stoop and deactivating the security system. He'd regret the honesty later. "More of an acquired taste. Like vodka."

"Sure. Compare violence to vodka."

"That's a lot of criticism coming from a pro football publicist." Joaquin moved ahead of her through the corridor. Off-hours LED bulbs dimly lit their path deeper into the gym.

In an effort to accommodate Joaquin's rigorous training regimen without shutting the door on paying members, Jules had offered him unlimited after-hours access to the building.

Joaquin preferred this concrete haven when it was purged of other people and personalities, decorated in shadows, accented with echoing creaks and yawns. He hadn't wanted to share the solitude with anyone.

Except bringing Martha here had been vital. If they could rehash what had gone wrong in this space four Decembers ago, maybe she'd table her resentment and he could more easily persuade her away from whatever had given her the shot-to-hell reputation that had her job in jeopardy.

If his conversation with Marshall Blue had made anything clear, it was that the Las Vegas Slayers' sexy young publicist was one scandal away from severance pay and unemployment.

And she didn't know it.

Martha meandered to a row of weight benches, stopping at the nearest one to trail her fingers over the various-size plates. "Most kids' early memories of their parents include stuff like bedtime story readings or baking lessons. Mine include counting my father's reps on the weight bench and watching my mother practice her pageant walk."

"I thought Tem quit chasing tiaras when you were born. And didn't Marshall stop bodybuilding even before that?"

"True and true. But they're sticklers for maintenance.

Being beautiful or packing on muscles is hard, so why not reap the rewards for as long as possible?"

It made perfect practical sense.

"Pop can lift over two-fifty, I think. What about you?"

"I bench three-ten."

"That's…a lot." Martha turned away from the weight-lifting equipment. "You can hold almost three of me?"

"I'm finding one of you to be more than enough to handle."

Joaquin's unfiltered retort earned him the softest of smiles as she moved on to the ring, where she batted a pair of boxing gloves that hung from a bottom rope.

"Good news. There's only one. There'll never be another me."

He could agree that, nah, there never would be another woman whose absence in his life could drench him with both relief and grief. Before her, and after her, there would never be another woman he wanted when he had every reason to stay away.

"Violence isn't vodka, and boxing isn't football, Joaquin," Martha said, doggedly pursuing a point he thought they'd dropped at the door. She slapped the gloves together. "Football's more…dignified. The league—my own sister, even—is constantly researching ways to make the sport safer. We—we use *helmets*, for cripe's sake."

"Boxing gloves serve a purpose." He tugged the pair of gloves from her grasp and unwound them from the rope to set aside.

"A player would be fined, if not booted off our roster, for the assault I've seen you lay on a competitor," she continued, stepping over his argument as if it were trash on the street. "Anyway, I've caught only a few of your matches. Weren't all that memorable."

As the last word crept past her lips, Martha's gaze swung away from his. She was lying to him—and it cut clean through his ego to nick his heart. The last time they'd been together in this gym with the doors locked and the lights down, she'd been so honest that he'd barely been able to stand so much messy, screw-up-everything truth.

But in the years since, he'd faced so much deception that he was still feeling the aftereffects. Let her discount his victories as forgettable. At least then she could take a swipe at his pride without compromising her integrity.

Because liars, he neither trusted nor forgave.

A half turn brought him to her. "Respect me."

"Yeah? And tell you stuff you want to hear?"

"Tell me the truth." He rested his palm at the base of her neck. Martha's features tensed in protest for a moment; then, her eyelashes trembled softly as her lids closed. Surrender. "Rehashing this—it ain't gonna be pretty. Can you handle that?"

A fragile sigh escaped her lips with the stroke of his thumb up her throat. "Easy."

"Let's see how you do without flirting and jokes to hide behind."

A spark of something that had been absent a minute ago brightened Martha's eyes, as though she'd found inspiration in something he'd said. Grayish light illuminated her strut to the ringside stairs.

"Flirting got us to this point," she said. The sound of her skinny-heeled shoes on the steps reverberated through the room. Ducking between the third and fourth ropes, she invaded the ring. *His* ring. "We were in this square, right?"

Kneading his forehead with the heel of his hand—which did nothing to assuage the painfully seductive sight of Martha crossing the competition ring in ripped-up jeans and tall shoes—he answered, "If you want those kind of details, then, yeah, we were flirting in the ring."

"Uh-huh. *We.* As in mutual." She crooked a finger and he found himself taking the stairs with a little too much energy, and coming to her with a little too much power in his stride. "As in, part of you wanted me, Joaquin."

Wants, he almost corrected. Only by the grace of God had his common sense strangled the blunt confession.

Casting a languid look from his face to his pelvis, she grinned. "Thanks for the reminder, but I already knew exactly *which* part that was."

Joaquin had been half-hard from the moment Martha danced on his crotch at the hotel, and if she could tap into his current thoughts, she'd see an image of him drilling into her on the canvas. No soft beds. No candles. No fairytale seduction.

None of the things she had carefully planned for them four years ago, when she'd worked up a crush and had chosen her first Christmas home from college in New York to get to him.

If he'd paid enough attention to something other than his catapulting career and his crumbling relationship—supposing a *relationship* was what he'd had with India—then he would've seen that Martha was after more than the short term, more than sex he could lose himself in. Her attention, her presence, had consoled him out of the type of hell that provoked some men to seek comfort from the depths of a bottle or the contents of a syringe.

Martha sagged against the top rope, arching her spine. "What are you thinking?"

"One of us should've said no. It should've been me." Ten years her senior… Why hadn't he been wiser, instead of shortsighted, fixated on loss and lust and what her touch and taste could do for him?

"Said no to what?" she pressed. "Letting me in here that night? Or do you regret the time we spent standing here talking and laughing?"

Conversation had flowed so easily, drifting from one topic to the next, cresting into laughs that rang throughout the darkened gym, and ebbing into slow, relaxed pauses.

Martha pushed off the ropes and positioned herself

against a corner post. "C'mere. We do this accurately, or we don't do it at all."

"I hadn't laughed, cracked a smile—none of it—in weeks," he recalled, advancing toward her in a few careful steps. As he had four years ago, he gripped the top rope on her left and the one on her right. "And you told the lamest-ass joke I'd ever heard."

"It was beautiful, your laugh," she whispered, pensive, her expression drawn in a frown. "So rough. Unexpected. I felt it everywhere. All over me."

"Then you put your hands on me, Martha."

She coiled her fingers over his forearms, her nails imprinting on his jacket. "I wanted to make you feel the heat I felt just to be near you."

Past and present collided, as her palms skimmed his arms. He'd lived this moment before, only there was *more*. More sizzle in his blood at the brush of her hands on his collar. More urgency in the crash of their bodies and his grip on her ass.

Joaquin rocked her against him. That night she'd been in a party dress, something fancy and silky. And when he'd touched her, the fabric had molded to her curves. Tonight, denim covered her flesh.

"Jeans." The word came out on a harsh exhale.

Studying her through the filmy overhead lights for a lengthy moment, not touching her, giving her ample time to slip out of the ring, Joaquin knew that the reenactment was an invitation to trouble. To be accurate, they would cross the line again…go too far again.

"What kind of champion waves the white flag for a pair of two-hundred-dollar jeans?"

Joaquin had a choice. He could interpret her comment as a snide remark to ignore, or a challenge that he needed to accept. Hooking a finger into the waistband of her torn jeans, he yanked her forward.

Eager. Impatient. Martha met him with a look of desperation so similar to what he'd seen this morning in the mirror when he'd let himself into the gym before dawn. Caught between awake and asleep, he'd tried to kick her out of his head. But she'd been too stubborn, too quick to catch.

Now she was too much like him, grappling for a full-body rush of pleasure.

Prying her hands from his jacket lapels, he curled them around the ropes again, pinning her flush against the post. Martha tipped her face back, offering her throat…yielding.

Could a kiss fulfill him? Heal him? Anxious, reckless, he bent, eclipsing her under the dull lights. Bringing his mouth down on her throat, he dived his fingers into her hair. The springy, feather-soft curls felt so good, he flexed his hands into fists, tightening his hold.

In response, Martha swayed against him. And when she moaned, he was ready. His mouth on hers, he caught the sound in a hard kiss. Plunging into her with his tongue, he could drink in her taste, swallow down her eager sighs.

"Your nose," she said when they parted once for air. "It's been broken before, hasn't it?"

"A couple of times."

"I've never kissed a man with a broken nose. Those men, they were storybook hot—not real-life, *scarred* hot."

"Then you've been kissing the wrong men, Martha."

Joaquin released her hair, but not her mouth. Eyes shut, he blindly let his hands navigate her body—the roundness of her tits, the taut line of her abdomen, the curve of her hips—until they met the front of her jeans.

Working the row of buttons free—yeah, there *would* be three to get past when he was all but feenin' to get reacquainted with her heat—he shoved the jeans and thong down past her hips. In tune with him, she parted her thighs and received his touch with a whimper that shook him from head to toe.

This part was different—her reaction, their connection. Working two fingers into her, and finding her tight but slick, he decided to give her pleasure that was different from the first time. Teasing her with only one brush of his palm on her sensitive flesh, he stroked into her. Faster. Deeper. More.

Martha broke away from his mouth. "Joaquin, I can't… uh…"

"Can't what? Come?"

Jaw tight, she said, "Yeah. Come. I can't, not this way. Not without—" She let go of the ropes and tried to bring a hand down to the bead of flesh that would take her to the top much too quickly.

But he batted it away, growling, "Again, you've been with the wrong men." He plunged in even deeper, drawing a gasp. "Put your hands on those ropes, or on me. You're in my ring, and right now, this is mine."

Martha cursed and took his mouth in a biting kiss that was barely shy of brutal, and he couldn't remember ever wanting her more. His body was in sweet torment, desperate for her hands, her mouth, but the release he wanted wouldn't come from burying himself in her. He wanted to be released from the guilt he'd carried since the last time they'd been this close. And if he couldn't have that, at least he could give her a sample of the ecstasy she thought she was incapable of experiencing.

"No lies, Martha," he groaned against her lips. "The rule's always in effect here. So don't fake anything with me. Want me to go faster? Even deeper?"

"No." She shook her head frantically. "Don't change a thing. Don't stop. This is perfect."

"I know. You wouldn't be so wet if it wasn't."

"Why'd you ask me, then?"

"Just wanted to hear you say it."

She dug her fingers into his shoulders. "Remind me to slug you later. Right now, prove that I'm with the right man."

Aside from sex, he certainly wasn't the *right man* for

her—and they both knew it. But he was the man to make her come in a way she hadn't before, and that had to be enough.

Strumming her, he watched, fascinated, as she slammed back into the post and screamed out her orgasm. The sound vibrated through the gym and flowed through him until her breathing started to even out again.

He withdrew, and she continued to tremble gently.

"It didn't happen that way," she finally said, staring at the hand he'd had between her legs, the fingers he'd had inside her. Then she searched his gaze. "We didn't kiss."

No, they hadn't. Four years ago, he'd peeled off her silky dress, kneeled and, with one of her legs thrown over his shoulder, feasted slowly. After his tongue's attention had made her climax, he'd tried to stroke into her and her body had resisted him.

And the realization had hit hard. She'd lied to him.

You're a virgin... The words had shot out as an accusation and, the selfish idiot that he'd been, he'd acted as though her manipulation had given him license to hurt her pride.

"I told you that I'd been with someone before," Martha said now. "I knew you would've backed off if you'd known the truth."

Oh, he'd backed off, all right. He'd demanded the full truth, found out that she'd booked them a hotel suite all set with rose petals and fancy candles and had hoped that he would say yes to driving her there and making love to her.

She'd said "making love" when all he could handle was sex. She'd been hoping for sweetness and commitment, when he'd been enduring life one day at a time.

Unable to see past the fact that she'd almost tricked him into taking her virginity, that she was yet another woman who'd lied to him, he'd harshly ordered her the hell off the gym's premises...off his territory.

I want a real *woman,* he'd snapped. *One who doesn't*

need flowers and candles. One who knows what to do with a man.

It sickened him to recall what he'd said, to remember her naked, vulnerable and heartbroken.

"I shouldn't have treated you that way," Joaquin said.

"You were in a bad place." Martha eased her underwear up over her hips, following with her shredded jeans. "You'd just broken off your engagement. Your suffering was my opportunity."

"No excuses." They weren't deserved or wanted. He shook his head, but the memories remained lodged there. "I'm sorry."

"Okay." Martha began buttoning up. "And about what just happened—"

"I'm not sorry for touching you. You deserve to feel that good, and often. But that's all I can offer."

"I was going to just say thanks." Martha lifted her brows. "Maybe the Martha of four years ago couldn't handle the reality of what we did tonight, but *I* can. I'm not a virgin anymore."

Joaquin bent and kissed her, even as he tried to warn himself against it. "In some ways you are. I just showed you there are still things you haven't experienced."

"Then the same could be said about you," she served back, climbing out of the ring. "You're a trust virgin."

"A *what*?"

"You never trusted anyone you claimed to love, even your fiancée."

"Turns out I was right, you know, since I walked in on her screwing my friend. After that, what'd she do? She tried to pin his kid on me." He'd lost time, money and a touch of his fans' respect when India had lured him into a public, drawn-out courtroom battle that included tampered DNA results and an unnecessary scandal that had done nothing but rip her credibility to shreds and leave her open to eventually lose custody of her baby to the kid's father.

"Yes, but you don't know what it's like to trust—really trust—someone. My love for you? Trust was built into it."

Martha's "love" hadn't been more than infatuation—he was convinced of that. But he didn't say so as he hopped out of the ring and walked toward the restroom to clean up.

"Joaquin."

He stopped.

"Do what works for you. I'm only saying that you haven't seen it all, lived it all." Martha hesitated, then traced his jaw. "And yeah, what happened here before doesn't matter anymore. 'Cause I'm not asking for a night in a hotel room. Just a ride home." Blinking, she let him go. "Get washed up. I'll wait by the door."

Chapter 5

Midnight rolled as the Escalade swung a left onto Opal Canyon Court. At the center of the cul-de-sac, Martha's house stood at the arc in the road, flanked by a scatter of gated, mountain-view properties. The street, canopied with trees and lined with wrought-iron lamps, was hushed, as it usually was this time of night. Aside from the occasional blare of music, the most noise Martha heard tucked away in this nook of town was the whisper of a gate opening and closing, and the yawn of wind.

Privacy was practically a guarantee—her sister's high-profile ex had chosen the property smartly. So Martha didn't feel especially nervous now about anyone getting a peek at her gates sliding open for a dark-windowed luxury truck.

Assuming that Joaquin would drop her off on the sidewalk and keep driving—putting her and what they'd done at Ryder's Boxing Club in his rearview mirror—Martha had started to push open the door to get out when he'd said, "I want to see you get inside safely."

It was the first exchange they'd had since leaving the gym. Martha, whose heart was still dizzy from the boundaries they'd burned in the boxing ring, hadn't known how to play things once they were inches apart in the vehicle.

"I have coffee." Right away, Martha winced at the inanity—no, stupidity—of the words. Of course she had coffee. So did damn near everyone in the free world. "I'm going to fix myself tea, but if you want coffee before you go, it wouldn't kill me to hook you up with a cup."

Teasing, "If you're sure it won't kill you, then yes, I'll take a cup," Joaquin brushed his knuckles down her arm, then unlatched her seat belt. "Lead the way."

Expecting these moments to be tenser, much more awkward, Martha wanted to drop back against the seat with relief. Instead, she kept her expression cool all the way from the truck to the house.

Why am I inviting this man into my house? she thought, shutting the door behind him and strolling ahead, knowing he'd follow. In the formal living area she turned, caught the sight of his sulky frown and the heat in his eyes, and was momentarily paralyzed with desire. *Oh, that's why. Because I haven't figured out how to stop being so freakin' hot for him.*

The kisses and the touches he'd given her in the ring had been nothing short of magic. The pleasure was drugging, and she was needy for more. But she wouldn't ask for it. He wasn't a practical choice for her. Not only would her parents rain down hell upon Joaquin and Martha if they found out what they'd done, but she didn't want to get wrapped up in hopes for a future with a man like him. His obsession with danger, his determination to base his value on how many times he could walk into pure violence and emerge victorious, scared her on levels she didn't want to admit.

Yes, she followed his career but played it off as though it bored her. It was better than owning up to fear that tore her to pieces every time she tried to watch him fight. It was *far* better than confessing that she was afraid for him, and was angry with herself because of it.

"Just give me a sec to change, and I'll get that coffee going," she said. He moved soundlessly, so close on her heels that she could smell the cologne she'd breathed in at the Foundation Room, in his truck and at the gym. Instead of carrying out her initial urge to dive onto the couch and shout, "Take me or get out!" Martha swept up a pair of remotes, twirled them like a Wild West gunslinger, and turned on the television and the electric fireplace.

Then she hurried to the kitchen before she could circle around to her first urge again.

Quickly, she dropped her purse onto the counter, put the brewer to work, fixed herself a mug of Irish tea and pried off her stilettos. The cabinet she dedicated to comfy foot-wear offered a variety of plush slippers, cozy socks and... clogs? Making a mental note to donate the clogs to charity, she pulled on a pair of polka-dot toe socks.

After arranging the coffee and tea on a tray, Martha real-ized she had no clue how Joaquin took his coffee. An hour ago, the man's fingers had been doing wonderfully dirty things to her body and sanity, yet she didn't know how he felt about cream and sugar in his caffeine. If her mother could scrounge up outrage that Gideon Crane hadn't known her middle name was Chastity, then how might she react to Martha and Joaquin's secrets?

"Not good," she mumbled, adding Truvia and Baileys to the tray.

Did it really matter that he'd been a stranger for four years and in under forty-eight hours had found his way back into her undies and her heart?

To the public, to the Blue family, it would undoubtedly matter, because it was a scandal waiting to unveil itself. But Martha found freedom on the fringes of convention.

Intuition had outweighed the old hurt, had compelled her to be daring enough to ride with him to the closed-for-the-night gym. It had felt beyond right to trust Joaquin with her body. His touch had told her things he'd never say.

Even if he wasn't hers—would never be—she cherished what he'd made her feel tonight. Hell, she cherished their banter in the truck and how deeply she'd gotten to him at Mandalay Bay.

"Thought you were going to change," Joaquin said when she padded into the living room with the tray.

"I did." She passed off the tray to him and wiggled her toes. The purple-dotted gray socks clashed with her outfit, but she didn't care. "My tootsies wanted to slip into something fuzzy."

"Those are some interesting socks."

"They make sense. Average socks are for toes what mittens are for fingers—constricting."

She took her tea mug and curled up on the club chair where she'd slept last night. The throw blanket over the back smelled cottony fresh and the sticky ice cream smear had been cleaned. She'd get the names of the staff her mother had rallied to tidy up and would keep them in mind when she hit up Anthropologie and Nordstrom for last-minute stocking stuffers.

Without bothering with sweetener or cream, or taking a moment to test his drink's temperature, Joaquin took a swallow. "Good coffee."

"It'd better be. It was imported from Brazil, and it was a pricey graduation gift from my sis."

"Which one?"

"Danica." Danica's gifts—whether it was coffee beans, a handmade garment or a mansion—were always considerate. Martha had spent so many years envying Danica's "perfect daughter" status that she hadn't realized her sister was more than a people-pleaser and Martha really should try to be nicer to her.

"And you're wasting this on me?" Joaquin set down his mug. Sweet hell, he was sexy.

Martha wanted to lick the coffee's unique berry-and-caramel flavor off his mouth.

"I don't think I'm wasting it," she replied, wiggling her toes and reaching over to rub a foot. "Ow. This is the painful cost of dressing up my feet with impractical shoes."

"And diamonds."

"You noticed my toe ring?"

"Isn't that why you wear it?"

"Nope, actually. I think it's pretty and wear it for myself. Just like my other body bling."

Martha took a hasty gulp of tea. *What* in blazes was she doing? Flirting with him like this before had led straight to...the most electrifying orgasm of her life.

The tremors had rocked her body, and though she was contented now, arousal was beginning to stretch inside her. Yup, her horniness was awakening from a catnap.

"What other body bling?" Joaquin's gaze blatantly fondled her. "You're pierced?"

"Obviously." She raked her hair to the side, exposing an earring.

"Where else, Martha?"

"That's for me to know, and you to find out—if I let you. New subject."

With a tight nod—the man really was a master of control, wasn't he?—he gestured to the shopping bags grouped near the sofa. "What's all that?"

"Stuff my mother brought this morning. Christmas decor. My undecorated house is an abomination."

"Are you going to put it up?"

"Maybe. Just another thing Tem can bulldoze me into."

"Sounded to me like decorating was something a mother wanted to share with her kid."

"Do *not* use that word in reference to me. I haven't been a kid for a long time and I don't need anyone to hover."

"You're Tem's kid. Marshall's kid. That's a privilege."

"I didn't go looking for the privilege, Joaquin. I was born into it."

Joaquin's parents hadn't loved him; they'd broken him. Martha knew that. She also knew he'd literally fought for everything he had. But his take on her relationship with Marshall and Tem didn't acknowledge that she'd carried her parents' resentment her entire life, and that hanging lights and trimming a Douglas fir wouldn't change things. Miracles like that didn't happen—not even at Christmas.

"Just hear this," he said. "If you want to face off against Tem or Marshall, wait until shit gets real."

"Advice you don't live by," she retorted. "Did you lose less significant matches to get to the main card? No. You won every fight and you're here in Vegas now because you intend to keep winning."

Joaquin's frown deepened, and she was puzzled that she could at the exact same moment want to slap him and kiss him. "Martha, dozens of times I've walked into a club and some asshole whose liquor made him too bold for his own good tried to get in my face. I've had to pass up the easy victories—the hollow ones—because they don't pave my way to a win that matters. *That's* why I'm America's champion. *That's* why I'm the best."

Martha's eyes narrowed. "Maybe instead of kicking it with me, you should go home now and work on your self-confidence. I don't think your ego's *quite* enormous enough."

She hadn't noticed that during their back-and-forth, they'd shifted closer. And now they were standing inches apart, and she was randomly annoyed that he wasn't backing down.

"I'm satisfied with my relationship with my parents. So, thanks, but no thanks, for the word of wisdom."

"What if Marshall and Tem aren't satisfied with their relationship with *you*?" Joaquin edged closer. "Tem was pissed when I showed up here this morning."

"Not because of some garland and lights. Because a guy spent the night."

"He's my friend, who spent the night along with two of my other friends, and he didn't come close to touching me the way you did in the gym."

A muscle jumped in Joaquin's jaw. Was he reliving every

second of pinning her to that post in the ring, of stroking her so, so deep?

"A man and a woman can be friends without having sex," she said. "Believe it or not, but I know that to be true."

"What's that supposed to mean?"

"People call me a 'party girl.' No, I don't live for the bad moments. Yes, I love enjoying myself. But I don't need a spreadsheet to keep track of how many men I've had sex with."

Well, she hadn't meant for that to go flying out into the open air, but her filter tended to malfunction when she was epically aggravated.

"Hey," he said, so gently she was momentarily confused, "who said that?"

"Not important."

"You're not that woman."

"How would you know? Before yesterday, you hadn't spoken to me in years." The same years she'd spent tracking his career, worrying about him even as she resented him, because, damn it, someone had to worry.

Her parents, her sisters, his uncle, his cousins, were supportive. Proud. But did any of them fear for his safety and wonder how they'd breathe again if they lost him?

"As much as the misconceptions sting, you're hiding behind them. And you're doing that to protect yourself."

Martha's grip relaxed. God, how she wanted to protest. Yet just hours earlier she'd lied to Tem, saying the reason she went "off the grid" was because she partied, when the truth was she burned the midnight oil studying more often than she did partying. She'd lied to protect herself...

"If you're going to do that, hide like that," Joaquin said, "think about how it reflects on the football team you represent."

"The Slayers franchise isn't your concern."

"If I owned a team, I'd want it to be a cohesive unit dedicated to business interests—including its reputation.

And if there was someone on my payroll who constantly attracted negative publicity, I'd ax them."

Scoffing, she carted the shopping bags to the sofa and dumped the contents onto the cushions. "Good thing you don't run the Slayers."

"Fair to say. But suppose the people who *do* run it think as I do."

Martha paused midway through stacking boxes of silver stocking holders that spelled the word *hope*.

Though not a member of the Slayers' HR staff, she had an educated guess of how many employees her parents had terminated since acquiring the ball club. The number who'd gotten walking papers during the season was staggering enough. Her sister Charlotte had been suspended through the exhibition games at the end of training camp for fraternizing with a fellow trainer, whose father had sold the team to the Blues and was now under investigation for misconduct. Then Danica had quit the organization altogether after the owners had rehired the scandalicious quarterback they'd ordered her to fire in the first place. Of course, the situation had been tangled by the fact that she'd fallen in love with him.

An office fling wasn't in Martha's future—she had no interest in complicating a professional relationship with one-time-only sex. But if her private life, which hadn't felt truly private since her parents' acquisition of Las Vegas's football franchise, was no longer independent of her professional life...

She was in deep shit—professionally speaking.

Her parents had the exact mind-set Joaquin described. Only they were blunter, more ruthless about it, which must be a winning formula, as the Slayers were invading the play-offs with just one loss.

Never would Marshall and Tem allow her to cross over to business operations if she approached them with a reputation sullied beyond repair. They'd keep her banished to S-Dubs forever.

Or… "Joaquin, what are their plans for me?"

The man sighed, cursed. "Keep you on a short leash until after play-offs."

"Until they can neatly eliminate me from the business, you mean?"

He stepped beside her, scooped up the stocking holders and moved them to the cathedral fireplace. "If your job matters, come out of hiding, Martha."

"Haven't you reached your advice quota for the day?" she tossed back, glad that she could still speak through anger.

"No, 'cause technically it's a new day." When Martha jerked around to glare at him, he was all cocky smirk and piercing eyes, and her ovaries somersaulted synchronously. "If I end up decorating your fireplace by myself, there's a hundred percent chance it's going to turn out ass-ugly."

A girl could get whiplash from how quickly he riled her up then turned her on. "All right. I'll bedazzle the mantel. But only the mantel and only if you give me a hand. You're tall enough to reach the thing without a stepladder."

"Got an aversion to stepladders?"

"My mother and I had a mini-argument about 'em this morning." She turned off the fire, then handed him a solid nine feet of flocked garland pre-beautified with pinecones, berries, ribbon and clear bulbs. "That's what you missed before you came in and stared at my booty."

Joaquin shifted the garland in his arms and bits of frosty dust stuck to his jacket's sleeves. He looked…embarrassed.

Great. He had the nerve to annoy her, make her come, annoy her *again*, and now he'd reached a new plateau of hotness.

"I—"

"To deny is to lie…" she said in a lilting voice.

"Wasn't going to." He began to stretch out the garland.

"I was going to say that I'd stare at your booty for hours, if I didn't have to fight."

Have to? Joaquin didn't have to fight any longer—at least not from a financial standpoint. Her father had steered him toward shrewd investments and that was on top of the wealth he'd accumulated boxing professionally.

He was rich. He had a name. He no longer risked his life in the ring for those reasons… Did he fight simply because he didn't know how to stop?

"How do you gear up to walk into hell like that?" she asked after a while. They'd worked in quiet, with ESPN prattle filling the silences between the occasional "Hand me that over there" and "Move that this way."

"Drills, running, jumping rope, getting in the ring and practicing as if a championship's on the line every time," he said, stepping backward to see if the trio of crystal candle-holders achieved the symmetry she'd asked for.

Walking back, Martha examined the fireplace critically and finally nodded, satisfied. "Besides exercise," she said. "And besides scoping out the city where you're going to fight."

"Mind games help." He grinned at her curious expression. "I go through with the interviews and promo, but eventually I tune it all out. I pretend that I've never won a match, that I'm fighting for my life. That my opponent stole something from me, and the only way to get it back is to go through him."

"Sounds brutal."

"When I fight, Martha, it's art." Joaquin peeled off his jacket, gave a rough swipe at the garland debris stuck to the fabric and flung it over a nearby ottoman. "Technique is the fine line between brutality and art."

The words were laced with a subtle warning: *don't try to convince me otherwise.*

But could she? She knew more about bodybuilding and football than other sports, but she wasn't ignorant when it came to boxing, wrestling and mixed martial arts. She knew that he was a pair of gloves, a few technical rules and a dash of luck away from a cauliflower ear or worse.

The dangers of what it took to win a fight, and—God forbid—what it might take for him to lose, frightened her. That it all seemed immaterial to him saddened her.

He understood violence, was comfortable with it in ways she couldn't fathom. And yes, he was a trust virgin. Those details intertwined and made her heart ache for him in spite of how thoroughly he'd damaged it before.

"Joaquin, suppose I'd let you stare at me for hours. Would you still fight?"

"Yes." No hesitation.

"What if I told you where my other piercing is? Would you fight anyway?"

"Absolutely. I'll fight until I face an opponent with the physical credentials to outclass me." He retreated to sit on the sofa. "Oh, and when I find out where you're pierced, it's not going to be because you told me."

"*When?* Ha, ha."

"Forget that a couple of hours ago my fingers were inside you and you were moaning for me?"

The words, the tension behind them, gave her a wicked chill. "I think I can recall that," she managed to say, treading cautiously. "About the mantel. It's not ass-ugly. I doubt even my mother will find fault with it. Thanks."

"I just followed your orders. I happened to be where you needed me to be."

Yeah. *This* time he'd been there when she needed him. But how many times had she needed him, only to find a hole in her life where he used to be?

The man couldn't be relied on. No matter the good times, his apologies and their cat-and-mouse games, she had to protect herself.

Martha sat on the floor near his feet, facing the fireplace. "Now that space has character. It's how a fireplace should look, with personal touches on the mantel. It's meant for a family. This whole house is."

"You're going to hang up your dancing shoes and start a family?"

"Who says I'd have to choose?"

"Guess you wouldn't, but I'm picturing you pregnant and doing that stripper dance you were working at Mandalay Bay and it's—"

Martha peered at him over her shoulder. "What, ridiculous?"

"Concerning. And hot."

She snorted. "Right. Well, this is a fairy-tale house and someday I'll have my happy-ever-after here. A wedding, a baby, eventually a puppy. Night after night of slow dancing."

"Slow dancing?"

Martha scooted around and lay back on the rug, propping her polka-dotted feet on the cushion beside him. "Uh-huh. Don't spill my secret, but I'm a hopeless eavesdropper. For years, up until I moved here, I'd spy on my parents slow dancing. One of them puts on music—jazz or Motown or opera—and they sway in each other's arms. I watched them every chance I got. It's what I miss most about not living with them anymore."

"They love each other."

"It's so simple, the way you just said it. But what they have is… It's like a storybook fantasy that transcended into real life. Almost too beautiful for our world—you know, for people like you and me."

"You have a shot at something like that," he told her. Clearly he didn't think he did.

"Not yet, but someday." She could hope for someone to bring to family photo shoots and someone to slow dance with at the end of the day.

"Then what do you want now?"

Martha closed her eyes, considering. "A foot rub."

Before her brain could compute what was happening, her feet were in his hands and he was shifting over to sit directly in front of her.

She opened one eye. "What are you doing?"

"Massaging your feet." His big, firm hands flexed one foot and she sighed.

Okay, he wasn't her route to happy-ever-after. He couldn't give her what she needed. But he was for damn sure her route to happy-right-now.

The spike-heeled shoes had hurt, and within minutes he was able to relax the tension from her muscles and tendons.

In fact, all over she felt...sated? Not quite. Warm, possibly. Aroused, definitely.

The moment Joaquin rested her feet next to him, she placed them on his lap and slid them back and forth.

"What are *you* doing?"

"Massaging you with my feet." She propped herself up on her elbows, watching her feet travel to his crotch. "Your thighs are so hard. But I think *this* is harder."

He groaned, rolling his hips, pushing a hand up his face to his scalp.

"Mmm." She caressed, quickening her pace, getting her first real impression of his length and girth. "Say my name."

His hands gripped her feet, guiding them over his erection. "Damn, Martha—"

"That's right. Just like that," she said. "Now moan for me." Her skin felt heated and her voice broke when she spoke, but she couldn't stop when all she could presently think about was leveling their playing field. Years ago he'd seen her naked. Hours ago he'd made her come. Always he took control without apology.

My turn now. I deserve this.

Martha's legs drifted open, and then he was down on the floor with her, kissing her, thrusting against her fully clothed…simulating what might happen if she relinquished control.

"Get off me," she said, breathless, moist between the legs. "I want to see you."

They stood and as he stripped, she tried to regroup. Leveling the playing field was one thing. Falling into complete, two-become-one sex was something else altogether. It'd be easy to pass off the reins to him. It'd be effortless to trust him in ways she shouldn't.

Loving him hadn't been a choice. More like an inevitability. More like gravity. In the wake of it she'd wound up hurt.

She was strong enough to take a stand against her own heart, and she wouldn't let herself love him again or let him make love to her.

Some mistakes even she wouldn't make.

Joaquin pushed his underwear down and Martha gasped softly. The size of him was…intimidating. How her inexperienced body might've accommodated him if things had gone the way she'd planned some years back, she had no idea.

She rushed him, laying her body against his, opening her mouth under his. "Can I—please?"

Crap. There she was being vulnerable again. Something about him caused her guard to slip every time. But in a matter of weeks, his fight would be over and he'd be gone again. Back to Miami or somewhere else entirely.

For tonight, this moment, she had America's sexiest fighting champ naked and ready to bang her to oblivion.

Joaquin eased back, swept up his pants and produced a condom from his wallet. "Here."

Martha took it and flicked it aside. "Won't be needing that."

He wrapped her hand around his shaft, moving it roughly up and down. "I'm not putting this in you without a condom."

"Fine, because I thought we'd do things a little differently," she whispered, tightening her grasp, slowing her stroke. She glided her other hand up his abdomen to his chest. Everywhere were firm bulges and ropey veins. He was flesh, bone and steel—she was certain of it.

Settling her lips on one nipple and exploring the other with her fingertips, she let his groans fill her. "Liking this?"

His hands snaked into her hair. A swear, then a muttered, "You know I like it."

She unwound his hands from her hair and started to lower. "And if I sucked you off? Would you like that, too?"

"Open up," he snarled.

"With pleasure." On her knees, she clasped him and traced a raised vein with her tongue before closing her lips over him. Earlier tonight he'd taken her by going a bit deeper every time. She now took him in the same fashion.

Rewarded with the feel of his body shuddering in reaction, she kept worshipping him with her mouth.

"Martha..." he said, easing out.

She scraped her teeth lightly over the tip of his flesh before letting him go. "Can I confess something?"

Joaquin dragged a palm over his damp forehead. Oh, yeah, she could definitely make him sweat. "What?"

"I've got my own selfish reasons for doing this." She trailed kisses down his shaft. "I like the weight of you in my mouth...the texture of you on my tongue. I like knowing that what I do can break you down. It doesn't matter how savage you are in the ring, because my touch can make you weak. It reminds me that you're human underneath it all, and I need that reminder."

Joaquin's fingers dug into her shoulders when she grasped him again and firmly pumped. "Where do you want it, Martha?"

The harsh whisper sent an arrow of delicious shock down her spine.

"The couch? The floor?"

Martha was close to panic for a split second. She *certainly* wouldn't ask the cleaning staff to return for a touch-up, and though she had club soda stored somewhere in the house, she wasn't going to spend the next hour scrubbing a rug. "No..."

Crouching for a kiss, he said, "Your pretty red sweater?"

"Favorite sweater, so that would be a no." Martha reached up to touch her lips to his jaw. In the hotel she'd wanted to kiss him sweetly like this, and now that she'd found her chance, she felt a half step closer to fulfilled. But she was still hungry.

And dropping down to welcome him back to the heat of her mouth, she loved him with tongue and lips until, with a yell and a tug on her hair, he poured into her.

She swallowed, draining him, stripping him down from a fighting god to an imperfect man, yet he was still strong enough to draw her easily up into his arms. Hugging her with affection disconnected from the dirty rawness of what they'd shared tonight, he stunned her.

Because she was reaching out to him, and she—Martha Blue, the woman who never came back to any man for seconds—realized she wanted another night like this with him, and soon.

Bad idea.

Squirming free of his embrace, she pushed away the messy emotional aftershocks. Just because she was sensitive didn't mean she wanted to be. She'd gladly trade emotions for something useful and less problematic, such as cooking prowess. "*Now* we're done."

"Done?"

Martha circled him, smacking his ass. "Get dressed, champ."

"What the hell—"

"Okay, okay. Everything I asked for that night, you denied me. I wanted to kiss you and taste you and be made love to. Denied, denied, denied." She licked her lips, swollen now and still stinging from stretching around his flesh. "But tonight I got that kiss, that taste—"

"I didn't make love to you the way you wanted."

Martha picked up the condom and his pants, and shoved the condom into a pocket before tossing the pants to him. "Got the impression you would've, if I'd allowed it."

She couldn't possibly look her best now, disheveled and flushed with mussed hair, but she offered her most radiant smile as he yanked on his clothes. Attractiveness was a formula comprised of sex appeal, perception and confidence. "Go now. I have work to do."

"After what we… You're going to work?"

"Yes. If I'm going to be an indispensable Slayers employee, I can't leave any slack. Your unwanted advice penetrated. Well, your advice and other things."

Joaquin laughed, taking her all the way back to a night four years ago that had ended so differently. The sound rocked her almost as thoroughly as his touch had.

A tinny rap song pierced the laughter, and Martha turned toward the kitchen, where she'd left her phone. "My friend's flying out to DC. This late, she's probably bored numb and dialing everyone in her contacts list to see who'll pick up," she said, jogging off to nab the phone. "A sec, okay?"

Plopping onto a stool at the counter, she plucked her phone from her purse and saw Leigh's name on the display.

She wanted to check up on her friend, whose comic relief she'd come to depend on…but she also wanted to say good-night to Joaquin.

It wasn't that she had expectations, or even hopes of a repeat of tonight. She just wanted another private moment before he returned to his world and she returned to hers.

She practically ran to the living room—but Joaquin was already gone. The mug he'd drunk from was on the coffee table, traces of his cologne in the air and his touch imprinted on her, but he'd walked out.

"He left." She wanted to be glad. She *had* to be glad. Because another electrically charged glance, another brush of his skin on hers, another tension-slicing laugh between them, and Martha would've asked him to stay.

Chapter 6

The evening crowd had already surfaced, throwing Las Vegas into nightlife mode in the middle of the afternoon. Pre-Christmas traffic had given Martha barely enough time to scoot home from the stadium, freshen up and get back on the road by four. The pizzeria where she'd agreed to meet her friend for an early dinner was located downtown, but nudged just off the Strip. Finding a place to tuck her Audi was an adventure she hadn't needed.

The day had been stressful enough, highlighted by drafting press releases about the team's divisional playoffs promo, sweet-talking a casting director and a record label into *encouraging* their big-name clients to attend the team's January celebration, and enduring a long-winded marketing and PR pitch to feature the Slayers' active roster in a PSA for safe sex practices. The pitch had wrapped up after devoting over twenty minutes to debunking sex myths. It had ultimately been decided that the Slayers—several of whom were young fathers and had at one time or another been the center of baby-daddy drama—weren't the best candidates for a PSA that emphasized the value of "No glove, no love."

Afterward, it had been hilariously appropriate for Martha's friend Chelle to suggest that they hit up the best naughty pizzeria in the city. Soixante Neuf was owned by a pair of Parisian artists who'd set up their restaurant below a tattoo parlor, decorated the walls with erotic paintings—available for purchase with the right attitude and at the right price—and applied a delectable French influence to Italian cuisine.

No one patronized Soixante Neuf for a family dining experience. Martha was peachy with that, because she'd be spending most of the evening in a PG-13 environment at Faith House. The youth center kept its doors open later during the winter holidays and summer months, which must be when Vegas's teens found themselves with more opportunity to dive deep into trouble.

Idle hands and all that, she supposed. Whenever she'd landed in a particularly sticky situation, her parents would blame boredom, and just like that she'd be plunked into a new hobby—until, of course, she'd *bored* her way out of it. Archery, horseback riding, oboe lessons—*oboe!*—and that painfully tedious etiquette seminar taught by one of Tem's debutante friends. The only enjoyment Martha had found in being schooled into a proper young miss was having her mother near, even if Tem had been more interested in spotting faults than supporting her daughter. But Martha was neither graceful nor inherently polite, and Tem had soon dazzled her to distraction with luxury-hunting.

Sophistication, precision and often a private jet made the difference between pedestrian shopping and Tem-style shopping. Day visits to Vancouver, weeklong antiquing trips across Europe, holidays spent roaming London for fashion inspiration or Mumbai for home decor. Gilded storefronts offering extravagant window displays, and store after store of shiny gadgets, sparkling jewelry and glamorous clothes had fascinated Martha.

But Tem's words had made a deeper impression. *My pretty girl. Nobody's perfect. Some can get close, but others fall far behind, like you. If something can improve you—can make you feel more beautiful—make it yours.*

And Martha, the quick study that she was, had taken fast to the hunt. She didn't have idle hands while swiping credit cards and balancing her checkbook. Shopping had become therapeutic and as a stress-reliever, it was a favorite. Not *the* favorite—that title she awarded to the after-dark sex play she'd had with Joaquin a few nights ago.

You'd think that knowing the man's hands were dangerous would've warned her that they might threaten her common sense. That they could turn any spot on her body into a pleasure point.

That they could confuse her into thinking she wanted more than a little wild fun, a bit of light risk.

Martha tugged open the heavy door to Soixante Neuf, comforted to be in a situation where she knew exactly what she was after. "Belgian Red," she said to the waitress who always greeted her with a chipper "'Sup, *cher*?" Avoiding the door traffic and the busy bar, she decided to wait for her beer at the plate-glass window that offered a view of the kitchen staff.

"Scootch over, Vine. You're hogging the window." Playfully she nudged Chelle, who was pressed up against the plate-glass and ogling a man with dark olive skin and slicked hair.

"Could be a matter of opinion, but there's something pervy about the way Enzo's fixing my pizza."

Martha looked on as the man finished spreading Soixante Neuf's signature sauce on a thin wheat crust.

Slathering sauce on a crust wasn't something she would normally call sexual, but if anyone could make a routine task seem like a sex act, it was Enzo.

"I wouldn't say *pervy*—" Martha started, only to be mesmerized to silence as Enzo sprinkled mozzarella, then arranged pepperoni slices in the shape of a penis. "Oh. Definitely pervy." She glanced at her friend. "I can also say the same about how your décolletage is pressed against this window."

Chelle staggered back. "You're all buttoned up now, but your office getup was a step away from hoochified."

"It's not hoochified if it's couture." Martha's jeggings

and asymmetrical sweater were positively wholesome compared to the slinky number she'd worn earlier.

Nervously pulling her micro braids over a shoulder, her friend said, "Is it a crime to be interested in how my food's prepared?"

"No. *Except* I've never seen you plastered over the sneeze guard at the deli. Are you into him?" She returned to watching the staff, but could feel her friend's hesitation. *"Really?"*

"Could be."

"Just the other day I overheard you describe your type of man as black and bald. Our friend here doesn't fit that criteria." She didn't add that Chelle's *type* changed daily. Thin, tattooed, short, muscular, sensitive, abrasive—any and all men appealed to her. Or so she advertised.

Chelle shrugged, teasing, "Black and bald, sure. But Marshall's taken."

"One, you're right. He is, and always will be, taken. Two, don't even joke about having a crush on the boss, especially in front of the boss's daughter. Three…when are you going to give up lying?"

"Lying's easier."

"Chelle, what are you afraid of? Our franchise takes discrimination seriously. Marshall and Tem will have your back."

"I promised my folks things would be different—*I* would be different—in Las Vegas."

"But you're not. You're making yourself miserable pretending you are." Shortly after Martha had been given an office in S-Dubs, she'd found Chelle crying in a supply room, desperate for someone to confide in.

"I'm not like you, Martha. I can't *not* care what my family thinks."

Martha cared, all right. Only now she needed to show it, if she intended to cross over to the front office—or stay employed with the Las Vegas Slayers at all.

"Just think. Guy after guy, and not one has changed you. Because you can't rewire yourself—"

"Stop."

"You *can* respect yourself."

"After you, Martha."

Fair shot, she supposed. Since her graduation homecoming she'd been linked to dozens of men. But in truth she was so focused on business school—and keeping it a secret—that aside from a single episode of skinny-dipping sex with Gideon last summer, and her infuriatingly unforgettable night of foreplay with Joaquin, the only net protecting her from absolute celibacy was a glow-in-the-dark vibrator.

"Sex should always be a choice," Martha said quietly. "When I'm with somebody, it's because I *want* to be. That's self-respect."

"Okay, all right?"

"No, it's not. Forcing yourself into these relationships? Chelle, don't let someone else take away your choices."

"In the spirit of exercising my choices, I'm going to see what happens with Enzo."

"It's going to take its toll eventually. Stacking those lies up like a Jenga tower. They'll topple, sooner or later."

"Let it be later, because now I'm busy flirting." Chelle puckered up as Enzo glanced up at them on his way to the ovens.

"Y'all a couple of freaks."

"You say that like it's a bad thing."

"Perish the thought!"

A *tsk, tsk, tsk* broke through their laughter.

"Looks like the only way to stop you two from staring holes into our best cook's posterior is to get you to a table quick," Odette, the waitress who'd greeted Martha at the door, said, carrying a Belgian Red and a local-brand beer with a lemon wedge poking out. "Got a clean one. Mind sitting under the *Ménage*?"

A pair of head shakes answered, then the waitress guided

them to a sunken dining area and a red-lit table beneath an oil painting of two men and a woman that left very little to interpretation.

Nabbing a seat beside Chelle, the waitress asked, "Which of you's getting the X-rated pizza? Enzo doesn't cook those up for just anyone."

Martha pointed to her friend. "It's Chelle."

"Shell?" Odette asked, offering a hand decorated with a mix of stones set in gold and silver and leather. "I've seen you pass through here, but never did get your name."

"You got it fine. It's short for *Mi*chelle." Her broad smile was…inviting?

Blanking out the sultry holiday tune gushing through the restaurant, the aroma of flavorful food, the red light washing over their table, Martha sensed awareness crystallizing.

Odette plucked her hand from Chelle's. "What are you after, Martha?"

"This beer and a small deep-dish cheese pizza."

"No guy?"

"No guy."

"Ah…what could that mean?" Odette's plum-colored lips softened to an unmistakably hopeful smile.

Odette, with her Louisiana drawl, artsy tattoos, crimped blond hair, grunge style and sweet-as-molasses charm, wasn't the first woman to hit on Martha, and odds were she wouldn't be the last.

Sarcastically, Martha said, "Tabloids say I haven't worked my way through every eligible man in Vegas. I'm determined to keep going till I snag a Guinness World Record."

"Tabloids? I've smoked better mind rot." At Martha's quirked brow, she said, *"Smoked.* Past. If my blood was any cleaner it'd be saline. So, c'mon, tell me the truth and I won't give you a dirty look if you leave without tipping me."

"The truth is I don't date. But I'm intrigued with somebody. Chelle, pry your eyebrows off your hairline."

"Sorry, this is my I-can't-believe-what-I'm-hearing face."

"Well, he's zero good for me. Domineering. Straight-up rude. Gets on my nerves."

"But you want to do him anyway," Odette quipped.

"Uninhibitedly, creatively and acrobatically."

"Any chance another Belgian Red—on the house—will change your mind about a certain Cajun girl?" Odette twisted her index fingers into her dimples.

"No more than a beer will change your mind about men."

"God, Martha, you're such a heartbreaker."

"That's what they tell me."

"'Kay. So a small deep-dish cheese for you—" the waitress nodded at Martha, then she smirked at Chelle "—and Enzo's number for you."

When Odette left the table, Chelle glared at Martha. "Either you made up that stuff about this dude you're googly-eyed over, or you just dished some hot-off-the-press details to the waitress."

"Odette's a good waitress. And my friend."

"So you *weren't* lying. Name, occupation, glove size."

"Glove size?"

"Approximate works. It's said to be a reliable indicator of whether a man's well-endowed…or unfortunately so."

"Why not just ask for his condom size?"

Chelle bit her lemon slice and grimaced. "Um. Do you *know* his condom size?"

"Nope." That, she could say honestly. She knew from firsthand—first*mouth*?—experience that Joaquin was damn fortunately endowed and almost too much to take down. But Chelle hadn't asked her that, and didn't need to know that Martha had been too focused on getting flesh-to-flesh with the man to note the brand, size, material, whatever of his condom.

"Then if you had to guess his glove size…" Chelle led.

"Sweetie, that sounds suspiciously like a sex myth. I've had my fill of those, thanks to the PSA pitch at work."

"Then name and occupation."

The arrival of Chelle's risqué pizza and a slip of paper with Enzo the cook's digits on it interrupted the interrogation.

Martha picked a slice of pepperoni, nibbled thoughtfully.

"Mind?" her friend complained.

"I circumcised it for you." Pinching the neck of her beer, she asked, "Gonna call Enzo?"

"Yeah." But the word was preceded with uncertainty so thick it could've smothered them both.

"What if this pizzeria hook-up is the beginning of your great, wonderful love affair, Chelle?"

"Crazy girl said what?"

"Your epic storybook love? Happy endings?"

"That's on *your* agenda. And I don't boot men out of my life all day long, then dream about fairy tales at night. I don't defeat my own purposes."

"You're saying I do?"

"If your purpose is to have wedding bells and babies and a love story of your own, then, yes, you do." Chelle blinked up at the painting over Martha's head. "At first glance, that looks like tug-of-war."

Martha turned, craned her neck. "Naked tug-of-war. And get a load of what's being tugged."

"Hey."

"Hmm?"

"Sorry. About that whole 'defeating your purpose' criticism. It was a bitchtastic thing to say."

And accurate? Martha speared the thought. She didn't like the idea that she blocked her own happiness. How messed up was that?

And how could she let her friend do the same?

"The epic love story I was talking about—" she looked Chelle in the face "—I didn't mean Enzo."

"Who, then?"

"Odette." The name was there, as bold and vibrant in her mind as the woman was in reality. "I saw you smile at her the way you tried to smile at Enzo."

"And new subject starts now."

Martha wasn't going to reopen a discussion Chelle considered closed and classified. Not here, in a restaurant with a pizza between them that presented pepperoni arranged in the shape of a penis.

"Let's talk about your lust life. You have access to a stock of men most chicks can only daydream about." Chelle's eyes widened. "Like Joaquin Ryder. The media's calling him Las Vegas's prince. Only Vegas would declare a man whose fists are lethal weapons its 'prince.'"

Joaquin didn't fit Martha's idea of a prince. He was too rough-hewn, too scarred, too dominant. And for those exact reasons, to name only a few, she was drawn to him. "This city's synonymous with risk and gamble and winning. Who better to represent that than the cockiest undefeated fighter in professional boxing?"

"Cocky. Guess he's got to be, to say he'll retire when he loses a fight. As far as promo goes, it's brilliant. But is he serious?"

"Far as I know, yes."

"Wow." Impressed, Chelle started on her neglected pizza.

Worry braided Martha's stomach, and only by pushing Joaquin and his crazy risks out of her mind would she undo the damage.

Giving her phone a glance as Odette brought her hot, cheesy pizza, she said, "Would you to-go that, please? I have to bounce. Math tutor duty."

"Who's gonna keep me company?" Chelle said with an exaggerated pout.

"I'm about to take over the bar, *cher*. How about I relocate you there?" Odette offered. As Chelle nodded, the waitress added, "Enzo's due for a break."

"Actually," Chelle backpedaled, "I do have a thing. Across town."

"You *are* going to call him, right?" Odette asked, her eyes mystified under a canopy of shimmery gray shadow.

Mumbling some noncommittal response, Chelle guess-timated her bill, handed the waitress some cash, and split.

Odette glanced from the money to Martha. "I'm confused."

No, *Chelle* was. She didn't *want* to want Odette. Just as Martha didn't *want* to want Joaquin. But that's what attraction and love could be—unbiased trouble.

Days had passed since Martha had done anything to piss off her mother, drive her father to pop antacids or provoke a lecture from either of her older sisters, so she figured she was past due for an "Aw, crap!" moment.

It came when she swung into the parking lot at Faith House, strolled past security and almost collided, pizza-box-first, into her sister Danica in the lobby.

"Hold it, chief." Danica, who had a several-inch height disadvantage even in her tallest stilettos, spied the box, then rolled her gaze up to Martha's. "Soixante Neuf?"

"Dinner. A girl's gotta eat."

"That box isn't going in there." She gestured to the brightly lit interior sprawled behind a pair of glass doors.

"How many French students am I likely to pass on my way to the kitchen, anyway?"

"Sis," Danica said with a knowing smirk. "You figured out what *soixante neuf* means long before you actually studied French."

As aggravating as debating with Danica was, it had at least restored her hunger. Gooey cheese and zesty sauce occupied her thoughts. "I'm a half hour early, I'm hungry and will eat in this lobby if I have to."

"It really is good pizza." Defeat. Danica waved her toward the interior doors. "Straight to the kitchen, and be quick."

"Yes, Ma."

"I'm not her. Never could be." Not that it was for lack of trying. Danica, the self-appointed spokeswoman for Too Perfect to Be True, had been a remarkable imitation of their mother, until Danica's no-no affair with the Slayers' quarterback had blown that to pieces. The real Danica had some flaws, quirks and kinks—and was a hell of a lot more fun.

Martha might tell her so. Someday.

Logging in at the reception desk, she clipped on her staff ID tag. A knot of volunteers and teens advanced toward her, and thinking swiftly, she hid the pizza box with her satchel.

The newness—or novelty—of her hadn't yet worn off at the outreach center. People's fascination with her reputation, money and connections was something she didn't understand. For the Blues, wealth and celebrity came with voyeurs, liars and backstabbers.

Looking forward to a quick dinner then a few hours of exponents and factorials, grid paper and protractors, Martha retreated to the gallery-style kitchen.

Raoul, a grizzled man who was never seen without his do-rag and had tattoos for sleeves, nodded a greeting as he towed a stock pot to a cupboard.

"I've got a pizza to reheat," she said.

"Keep bringing outside food into my kitchen, and you're gonna hurt my feelings," he said. "Next time, call and I'll put together something."

Put together. If cooking was the art form that plenty of foodies claimed it to be, then Raoul—a classically trained chef who'd soon be leaving Nevada to open a spot in the South—was the Rembrandt of the culinary world.

"You spoil me, Raoul. Too bad there won't be many

next times." Faith House's HR folks had already begun the recruitment process for his replacement.

At the counter she nudged aside a stack of travel magazines to make room for her satchel, pizza and copy of *Vanity Fair.*

The magazines fanned out to reveal a worn United States road atlas at the bottom. The thing was vandalized with sticky notes marred with scribbles detailing flight itineraries and bus schedules.

"Planning a US tour—"

"That's *my* stuff!"

Martha recoiled with a pang of embarrassment, before she realized she'd done nothing out of line—technically. How was she supposed to know a fat stack of travel magazines and a ratty road atlas belonged to a kid she'd never met, who was rocking last year's fashions, a half-dozen piercings in one ear and a fishtail bun that might've been attractive had frizz not conquered it.

"Bring down the attitude, Avery." Beneath Raoul's sternness was an admirable note of patience. "Nobody here's the reason your foster mama's having a rough go."

Fosters, runaways, delinquents, addicts, victims— Martha had been introduced to them all through Faith House. Each child, each dark story, circled her heart and tugged.

"Avery's foster mama's a chef," he told Martha. "Got her break on a TV show and works in one of those celebrity chef restaurants on the Strip."

A battle between pride and melancholy raged on the kid's warm brown face.

Encouraging, "Introduce yourselves," Raoul left.

When the girl remained stalwart, Martha said, "Avery, I'm—"

"I know. *Everyone* knows who you are. Online you're trending as the 'sexiest heiress in Sin City.'"

For all her frivolity and hubris, it wasn't a label Martha

wanted. She didn't care how many Las Vegas heiresses were competing for the title. "I was going to say, 'I'm Martha Blue and I'm irretrievably nosy.'"

"I'm Avery Paige and I'm leaving."

"Or you can stay, if you think this kitchen's big enough for the two of us to coexist without getting in each other's way."

A soft huff, then Avery plunked down onto a stool, sending over a gust of air pungent with the scent of Faith House's commercial-grade antibacterial hand soap.

Did the kid soak her hands in the stuff?

Avery unzipped her hobo, took out a textbook and a jacket, and jammed her atlas and magazines inside.

The same sterile scent rose from the fabric. Had she used hand soap as laundry detergent? By "rough go" did he mean Avery's foster mother was struggling financially?

"Care for a reheated pizza?" she offered.

"Because I'm a hungry, pathetic charity case?"

Sparing the girl insult, she lied, "No, I've got late party plans and want to preserve my appetite. Seems wrong to throw out a perfectly delicious cheese pizza."

Avery eyed the box in front of Martha, smirked, but didn't comment.

"What's funny?" *Uh-oh.* "Can you read French?"

"My school takes foreign language seriously, so yeah, I know that *soixante neuf* translates to the number sixty-nine in English. Also, I can name just about every restaurant and bar in this city. Oh, and I know exactly what that restaurant's about."

Damn. Avery didn't appear offended or corrupted, but Martha felt at fault regardless as she reheated the pizza. "You're a food and drink know-it-all because your foster mother's a chef?"

"*Was.* She hasn't worked in a while."

"Laid off?"

"Cancer won't let her work. And the state's effin' labor laws won't let me work a real job."

"How old are you?"

"Thirteen." Avery gripped her textbook for a long, tense moment. Petite and slight, she looked barely ten in spite of her piercings and tough-girl frown. "Crap. Sorry. People don't like sad stories."

"That doesn't mean they shouldn't be told." Martha set a plate in front of Avery.

"My foster mom wanted me to sign up for math tutoring, but I'm here for cooking tips. I'm collecting from-scratch recipes."

"Can't help with the cooking, but math's the love of my life." Martha tapped the front of the book and her pampered, gel-polished fingernails contrasted with Avery's jagged nails and bandaged cuticles.

A biter.

"What's got you stuck?"

"Quadratic equations."

"Factoring? That can trip people up."

"Formula."

Likely the quadratic formula wasn't all that had Avery stuck. But if she could help the girl with that, it'd be a start. "Pencil? Notepaper? Let's do this. My shift hasn't started yet."

"I'm eating your pizza and taking all your time," the girl said hesitantly.

"I come to Faith House to *share* my time." Initially, the commitment had been part of some lesson Danica had wanted to teach her. But quickly the place and people had become a treasured part of her routine. "Crack open that book, chickadee. We have only a few minutes to get quadratic equations to make sense."

"Great." Avery gnawed on a thick chunk of crust. "At least something will make sense."

One problem at a time, Martha was going to help this

kid. "This," she said, indicating an equation for Avery to copy, "needs to be in standard form. So to make this term zero and transfer it to the other side, subtract."

The girl labored but identified the coefficients to plug the values of *a*, *b* and *c* into the formula.

"Two-*a* is the denominator for everything sitting above it there," Martha reminded when the girl neglected to attach the *a*.

"Right." Then she stopped, scrunching her face. "Martha, if it's plus *or* minus, how do we get the correct number?"

"Number—singular—is a misleading expectation. Finish calculating with plus, then calculate with minus. Remember, the goal is to find the two values."

The values determined, and added into the quadratic for confirmation, Avery beamed but quickly sobered. "Pure luck."

"Pure *learning*."

"So you're a math geek?"

"I understand math," Martha explained. "It's something I count on to make sense when it seems nothing else does. I have the bandwidth to tutor another student, and it'd be nice to add a girl to my list."

"Only boys signed up?"

"Oddly."

"Not when you remember that the girls are probably insecure and the boys are boys."

"Oh. Well, if you ever find yourself stuck—on an equation or anything else—tell me."

Avery hunched over her food. "Whatever."

Martha jotted her cell number on a corner of the notepaper. "I'd like to help. This is for you and your foster mother."

"I probably won't be sticking around much longer."

The travel magazines returned to the forefront of Martha's thoughts. "Are you running away?"

"As soon as I save enough money. You can't stop me, unless you stick me in juvie."

The honesty was harsh, but Martha weathered it. "Is someone hurting you?"

"No."

"Why run?"

"Nobody sticks around. Why should I?"

"Who left you, Avery?"

"My bio parents. My first foster family… God, I loved them." She closed her textbook. "They couldn't have kids of their own. I grew up thinking they'd always protect me. But they used IVF, got pregnant and gave me up."

"Your current foster mother—"

"Is dying. She can't protect me."

There was that word again: *protect.*

"Raoul's moving away, so there goes another friend."

"I may be a math geek heiress, but friendships are my specialty."

"Your life's about parties and good times. You won't be available to solve a thirteen-year-old brat's problems."

"The staff here cares about your safety. Call the hotline. Call the cops. Call me." Noting the time, Martha grabbed her satchel. "Maybe it'll help you to hear this, or maybe it'll just help me to say it, but I was…stuck…once. Just one time, in New York. I needed a protector and found no one there."

"What did you do?"

Blamed herself. Made a few stupid decisions. Lost herself in denial. But eventually— "I swore I'd never be that scared again."

Avery stared down at the phone number. She didn't say yes, but she didn't say no.

At Hadland Park, Avery stopped walking. The softball field was vacant, shadowed. Perfect. All the Christmas in the air, brightening a reality she knew to be much dimmer, was nauseating. Faith House was as merry as the department store window displays her foster mom, Renata, had taken her to see the day after Thanksgiving. Though chemo and radiation had zapped so much of Renata's energy that she hadn't the strength to prepare a turkey and trimmings, the next day she'd taken Avery out early for their last good day.

Memories of pushing through downtown crowds, sipping hot chocolate in foam cups, pointing out something insanely fancy and joking "Buy me that for Christmas!" were made, but felt too deep in the past.

A couple of days afterward, Avery had learned that because Renata's illness was "terminal," the state would be taking her again. It had been—what was the word that rude bitch social worker had used?—*imperative* that Avery understand the unlikelihood that anyone would assume any guardianship of an underdeveloped thirteen-year-old whose birth parents had been drug-addicted teenagers.

Yeah, she was screwed.

Or, she would be, if she didn't run. No one could take her if they couldn't catch her.

She'd leave before Renata could leave her first.

No one would miss her, anyway. Renata slept most days straight through. Her jerk of a son from Washington had put Renata's condo on the market and complained every day that Avery's presence deterred potential buyers. She was convinced that the people at Faith House welcomed her only because the founder was friends with her foster mom's TV chef boss.

Cynically, Avery thought of the number Martha Blue had written in her notebook. She was almost curious enough to dial and confirm her suspicions that the number was a fake. It probably belonged to a spa or a Thai restaurant or a pest control company.

"Pest control, yeah," she mumbled, digging the toe of

her worn tennis shoe into the ground before striding away from the park.

Glamorous women like Martha couldn't possibly give a damn about lost girls like Avery. By some freak accident, their worlds had collided.

A bus ride and a brisk walk brought Avery to the nearest supercenter, where she purchased a screwdriver and a doorknob. It was basic, brass, but it had a lock.

She'd skipped buying herself lunch for over a week to afford the doorknob. Now that she thought of the yummy pizza Martha had given her, she regretted not rationing it.

It was after nine when Avery returned to Renata's cookie-cutter condo. In her dreams, she'd cook her way to world fame and would live safe and happy-ever-after in a sprawling mansion.

Slipping into the silent unit, she closed the door slowly. An earsplitting pop beside her head had her ducking with a terrified gasp.

"Busted your ass." Patrick, Renata's son, snickered as he dropped a fork and shreds of a balloon then scratched his bearded chin. "You smell like smoke."

Not surprising. The corner where she'd waited to catch a bus home had reeked of cigarettes, liquor and weed.

"Screwing around on the streets now?"

"No!" Was he crazy? Sex wasn't on her radar. She'd never even kissed anyone—not that she'd tell him that. "I was at Faith House. You know, the place Renata sends me to so I don't bother you? Then I went to Walmart."

"To buy what?"

"Deodorant." Avery hated lying—it made her nervous to do it, no matter the circumstances—but had justified buying a stick of deodorant as a separate transaction in case Patrick accosted her with the third degree. With the doorknob and screwdriver buried in her tote, she held up a plastic bag.

"Where's the receipt?" he spat.

"In the bag."

Snatching it, he dug out the receipt, scanned it and dropped it back in.

Avery almost smirked in satisfaction, but had learned quick that Patrick didn't appreciate being outsmarted. Every time she succeeded in making him look like the jackass he was, he found a way to hand down a punishment, which she then had to cleverly find a way around.

When he'd disconnected her cell phone, she'd secretly bought a prepaid one. When he'd cut off her laundry access at the condo, she'd started hand-washing her clothes wherever she could find a sink and soap.

But when he threatened her, she felt trapped. *Stuck.*

"Out shopping while my mom's worried, huh?" Patrick cursed, flinging the bag at her. "Can't figure out why she hasn't unloaded you yet. Just stay the hell out of my way."

Gladly, creep! Wordlessly, Avery stepped around him. She froze at the towers of boxes cluttering the contemporary living room. "What's going on?"

"Rummage sale. Sort out your junk, but if you take too long, it all goes."

"How come you're doing this now? Listing the condo, putting our stuff up for sale? Renata's not dead."

Patrick cocked his head. The anger in his eyes resembled confusion. "Why did she take you in? You're not worth the government check."

Money. Yup, that made sense. Patrick wasn't visiting because his mother was sick, and definitely not because of the holidays. "All you're thinking about is selling off assets and cashing in her insurance policy."

This time, she thought for a breathless moment, *he's going to hit me.*

Patrick's lips flattened; his fists tightened. "Stay out of my way, Avery."

She did, escaping to her room. Back against the door,

she waited until she heard the front door slam before she opened her tote bag and got to work.

Switching the dark bronze knob for the brass one with a lock was a simple process. Only after she finished did she tiptoe down the hall, whisper good-night through Renata's door and return to her room.

Out of habit, she barricaded the door with her desk chair. Then she rifled through her bag and pulled out the binder she carried everywhere.

It contained pages of inspiration. Magazine clippings of lavish estates, designer shoes, automobiles, dog breeds, exotic dessert-and-wine pairings—anything that might fit into her dream future.

She retrieved the glossy *Vanity Fair* that Martha Blue had left at the youth center. Martha was pretty and interesting enough to be featured on the cover. Avery wanted to be snarky, but Martha hadn't acted like the crazy-wild picture the media painted. And it was hard to *really* dislike someone who dined at the coolest pizzeria in town and stomped quadratic equations.

About now she was probably partying it up with her famous friends, living the high-fashion and high-class life that Avery hoped she'd have one day.

Avery selected a few photos of amazing spring gowns, and added them to her collection. Someday she'd have this life. She had to get out of Las Vegas first.

After Christmas, she promised, sliding into bed with her shoes on in case she needed to climb the fire escape at a second's notice. She wanted one more holiday with Renata.

Some indeterminable time later, she heard the new doorknob jiggle. Bolting up, she suppressed her breathing... waiting. The lock held and the jiggling stopped.

After Christmas, she consoled herself. *After Christmas, I'm free.*

Chapter 7

Joaquin's publicity crew sold his morning to MGM Grand. At dawn he was giving a heavy bag in Ryder's Boxing Club hell. But when he was at a crucial point in his workout, his designer-suited cousins bum-rushed him out of the gym, instructing him to be at the resort by nine for an interview.

His promotions company had been stirring the pot since he'd made the decision to train in Vegas.

State-of-the-art gyms around the world were his to experience. Fitness companies were vying to sponsor him, to persuade him to use their products, to link the success and hype of his name to their corporate images. But he'd already achieved physical perfection—if not surpassed it. His body wouldn't win, or lose, this fight. His *mind* would.

Survival, freedom, self-worth—he'd found it all through hellish bouts in his uncle's gym until he'd learned to brutalize his way to undefeated professional victory. As long as he stayed on top, he could survive, be free, trust that he was worth something beyond money.

No media tactics would carve that truth out of him. Shit, every mortal had a weakness. That he protected his made him indestructible.

The key was to give the faces behind the cameras and microphones only what he thought they deserved—and leave them feeling fortunate to get even that. His ex-fiancée's desperate campaign to corrupt his name and dive into his fortune had shown him how fickle the press could be.

After a solitary drive to the Promontory Ridge place he'd scarcely visited since settling in Miami—save for a few videoconferences with the middle-aged husband and wife who lived in the guest house and were in charge of the main house's year-round upkeep—Joaquin showered and put on armor.

The H. Huntsman suit and Bettanin & Venturi shoes weren't armor. Nor the cologne a boxing-enthusiast fragrance chemist had formulated specially for him or the diamonds-and-steel wristwatch he strapped on. His armor was an invisible guard, the psychological barricade that encased his emotions.

A man couldn't take on the role of Las Vegas's prince and not expect fanfare. He couldn't represent America without wearing publicity like raven's wings. But he for damn sure had to classify emotions as fuel for the fight, not media feed.

A single bodyguard accompanied him to the stocked and loaded Porsche limousine idling in front of the estate. With a pair of trusted law enforcement professionals stationed stoically opposite him, and the driver an intercom summons away, Joaquin almost immediately began to crack under the heaviness of silence. The drive to MGM Grand left him with too much time and opportunity to think.

Remember was more accurate. Losing even a drop of control with Martha wasn't wise. But he'd relinquished more than a drop when he'd put his hands on her in the boxing ring…when he'd let her use her mouth to take exactly what she wanted. She'd felt so good—the feathery softness of her curly hair, the greediness of her fingers, the silk of her lips, the slick velvet of her tongue—but all he'd done was reveal his weakness.

All he'd done was shown himself how much he wanted her. Own her body with his hands, and let her lay a claim on his—he wanted that and more.

It was the *more*, the below-the-surface stuff, that sent

his brain "Oh, shit" signals. Getting each other off, favor for favor, the way they had that night was hot…but it wasn't the sum of what he needed.

Martha's words, how she'd handled him, had stirred his mind. Part of him was grateful that she'd been so controlled, and that he'd left her house when he had. The other part wanted *more* with Martha—was darkly curious to see how naked they'd have to get, how deep he'd have to go, to find what hid beneath sexual demand.

Because something else was there—something that might conquer him if he didn't drag his ass out of its path.

"Well, I'll be damned," he muttered.

Both security guys snapped fully alert. "Problem, sir?" one of them asked, his voice smooth and cold as a sheet of metal.

"No. Just figuring something out." Something Martha had already suspected. She'd said he would've made love to her if she'd let him. She knew what they danced around was serious and a step from irresistible. Enticing her to ignore the warnings and take lust a little further, risk a little more, would be selfish if not heartless.

He cared about her too damn much to initiate that kind of hurt.

No. No, no, hell, no. He needed to derail that train of thought, quick. Using the hands-free intercom, he asked the driver for an ETA.

"Our car's arriving in another seven hundred yards," the driver reported. "The other cars have arrived at the destination."

By now it should be tradition that an event warranting one limousine would include an extra two rides. One car was the decoy used to help his group gauge the crowds and paparazzi and identify any threats. The other typically carried his entourage: security, Uncle Jules, Tor and his wife, and Othello and usually a few interchangeable conquests who he wanted to excite with a limo ride and a tease of celebrity treatment.

It all attested to Joaquin's success, so the hassle of it was his cross to bear.

When they turned onto Las Vegas Boulevard, he surveyed the streets through the car's tinted glass. Strands of people—some lugging shopping bags, a few saddled with children and too many brushed with that uniquely tourist awestruck expression—hurried toward MGM Grand.

In the time it took the driver to expertly park between the other two limos, the pedestrians congealed into a tight cluster that was directly parted and muscled aside by hotel security.

"Ever get sick of this?"

Reaching for his sunglasses, Joaquin glanced at the pair of security experts. He wasn't sure which had posed the question, but the honest response was ready. "Constantly. The way I see it, there're two choices. Resist the crazy or become it."

The three exited the limo as a woman shouted Joaquin's name over the noise and flashed her breasts.

"Or," he added lowly, shifting subtly away as hotel security approached her, "third choice. Ignore it."

"See what you mean." The shorter of the two men shook his head as he carved a path to the hotel's lobby. "Jesus."

Smiling wasn't Joaquin's forte, but the handful of phone-toting people he paused for didn't care as they grinned wide and clicked. From what he could glimpse behind him as he and his guards approached the building, his cousins were flaunting and boasting enough for the group.

Joaquin noticed Jules wasn't with them. Once inside the lobby, he went to Tor. "Where's your dad, man?"

"Last minute he said he was going to hang back at the gym. A service tech's coming to check out the plasma in the staff room." Tor gave a blasé shrug and drew his wife, Brit, close. "You know he's got no beef with this side of things, but he's more about the day-to-day stuff. Preparation."

"The fight."

"You know it."

Yeah, Joaquin knew it. On many levels, so was he.

Tor cuffed his shoulder. "Brit and I are going to soak up some of this VIP hospitality. Unless you want us hanging around for your close-ups?"

"Screw you." Video-recorded interviews were never favorites for Joaquin.

At his house, he'd called his publicity manager, who'd explained that the venue had made numerous concessions for the promotions company. The interview would be in a private section of the hotel and he'd be released by afternoon. His entire party would enjoy a full day of complimentary luxury as a thank-you for his cooperation. He was ready for the questions and cameras when the polished hotel concierge introduced him to a network television journalist and production crew.

Publicity folks and security patrolled the area, but he had no trouble pushing them into the background the way he tuned out any other audience as a pair of makeup artists attacked the years-old scar on his right cheek.

Afterward, he let photographers pose and direct him for a series of shots. Then he and his people migrated to a conference room, where he accepted a Bacardi from a server and sat down with the television journalist.

"Eliáš Brazda has two career losses," she began in a modulated voice. "Describe how his stats affect your confidence, facing him at the Garden Arena next month?"

"Brazda's losses affect Brazda," he replied. "Do they make him insecure? I don't know. Make him hungrier? I hope so, 'cause I want a hungry opponent. But his losses don't touch me."

"Are you confident?"

At this, the entire room vibrated with laughter. Confidence, he had that in spades.

"Gotta be." He tasted the Bacardi. "If I'm carrying doubt, then I shouldn't step into that arena."

"Let's talk nicknames." She chuckled. "Las Vegas's prince. Sinner. You've carried 'Sinner' for the bulk of your fighting career. What's behind it?"

If she was fishing for backstory, she'd picked the wrong bait. There was nothing sentimental or charming behind the name. "I'm a bastard in the ring. That's who ticket holders and pay-per-view subscribers see when they watch me fight."

"Do you fight to entertain?"

Joaquin paused, digesting the question. "I fight," he admitted, "because I'm a fighter."

The reporter studied him, considering. "You're also an investor for a Fortune 500 company, BioCures West Energy Corp. Your mentor, Marshall Blue, is primary shareholder. Recent press releases indicate interest in alternative energy sources—radical move for a rather traditional natural gas and electric provider. What can you say about that?"

Maintaining relevance and adopting an environmentally responsible worldview weren't radical. "Adapt or fall," he said. "Survival of the fittest applies to industry. Boxing. Public service. Journalism."

"The element of surprise. You're good." She breathed out a laugh. "Perhaps that's why you've never lost. At this point in your career, you can retire whenever you'd like. If Eliáš Brazda outclasses you at the Garden Arena, will you fight again?"

"The night I'm outclassed is the night I cease to adapt. The night I fall is the night I fail. When I fail, I stop being worthy of the ring."

When I fail...
Joaquin's words followed him out of the hotel's confer-

ence room after the interview. Would he ever truly be prepared to give up the fight—even when there was no longer any fight in him?

Left to his own devices, he unknotted his tie and went in search of something stronger than the Bacardi he'd left half-full.

Not yet ready to round up his folks, he avoided the casino. At every turn were holiday reminders: festive lights, pine and cranberry in the air, orchestral interpretations of Christmas tunes. For him, Christmas would be a training day that he'd begrudgingly cap off with an appearance at the Blues' Christmas dinner. A soiree, Temperance Blue's personal assistant had called it when she'd invaded his uncle's gym the previous afternoon to give him a fancy invitation tied with sparkly twine. Jules and the cousins had received theirs, and RSVP'd, back in November. Put on the spot in the gym, he'd set aside his jump rope and opened the damn invitation in front of the PA, who'd stood there expecting an answer to parrot back to Tem. So he'd agreed to come.

He would stay long enough to compliment the hostess and have a drink with the host. But he didn't see himself sopping up the full effect of a Marshall and Temperance Blue spare-no-luxury party.

He didn't want to imagine himself catching glimpses of Martha with some storybook date—a man pretty for her to look at, but who'd be too lazy or clueless to make her come screaming.

Besides, he'd grown up in Jules Ryder's household, where money was tight, practicality ruled and Christmas was rarely celebrated.

There had never been magic to the Christmas season. And he wasn't expecting there to ever be.

With security lurking like stealthy shadows, he sought the Lobby Bar. It was jammed with patrons but he wasn't deterred from ordering something top-shelf with burn.

Accepting the drink, he tossed a glance across the bar and saw Othello leaning on his elbow and staring at his phone with two glasses in front of him.

"Downing cocktails two at a time, cuz?" he greeted, joining the man. "How hard did the table games hit you?"

Othello straightened. A trace of a frown pulled at his mouth. "I'm still standing."

"Good enough."

"Wrapped up early, everything did, huh?" Othello scratched his chin.

Joaquin instantly thought, *Oh, hell. Now what?* because the index-finger-on-chin scratch was the nervous impulse that told table game dealers when Othello was bluffing the same as it revealed to his ex-wives when he was lying.

"Got out early on good behavior."

"You? Never."

"Funny." As he raised his glass, he noticed Othello scan the Lobby Bar. Whatever Othello stepped in, Joaquin wanted no part of it. The way he saw it, the road of life had plenty of shit piles and you could either dodge 'em or ride through 'em.

It was the kind of lesson a man figured out for himself.

"Let me get ahold of your driver, bruh," Othello said. "Tor and I are holding things down. Get back to your workout."

Road of life. Road of life. Joaquin wanted the words to motivate him to leave the bar, but he braced himself for the answer to "What'd you do?"

Othello gave an incredulous, offended scowl. "The hell?"

"I'm not in a playing mood," he warned quietly.

A pair of feminine hands suddenly covered Othello's eyes and behind him a woman's voice dared, "Guess who's not wearing panties?"

Oh. God. No. "Ciera Byron," Joaquin said, killing their verbal foreplay.

The hands released his cousin, and peeking out from behind Othello's shoulder was the same copper-haired woman Joaquin had ordered out of his Miami place barely a couple of months ago.

In a thin dress and pencil-skinny high heels, she teetered around Othello to glare at Joaquin. "America's most narcissistic athlete. Still got that controlling God complex?"

"You still have the tall shoes and a dirty mouth, but where's your sewing needle?"

"Asshat." Ciera bristled under the heaviness of his controlled anger. "I'm not getting in the middle of a brawl. Call me later, O."

"Good to see you, too, Poker," Joaquin said.

"Brute," she tossed back, sauntering past.

"I liked *asshat* better." When she all but stomped down the steps and out to the hotel lobby, he said to his cousin, "*She's* your casino hookup?"

"Man, look. I thought you'd take off after the interview."

"And you'd show Ciera a good time? Glad I could help you get that opportunity." Had Joaquin not been Mister Cooperative this morning, the hotel wouldn't be rolling out all-day luxury for his entourage. "Ciera? *Ciera!*"

Othello glanced around surreptitiously. "She said you'd make this about you, but I'm here to tell you it's not."

"It's about Ciera, who's a liar. A schemer. I cut her out of the circle after what she did in Miami. Tell her there's no way back in. Not even through you."

"Don't be like that. We're cousins. We're tight."

"Don't play the family card when you're screwing my ex-girlfriend." Joaquin considered the contents of his glass. "Answer this, man. When you visited Miami and I introduced you to Ciera, did—"

"No."

"Let me ask the question, Othello. Did you touch her when she was mine?"

"No," his cousin said again. "Ciera approached me at a

concert here in Vegas a few weeks ago. She said she was in the city on business. I gave her a reason to stick around."

Ciera was a buyer for a department store chain. Possibly what had sent her across the country the same time as he was preparing to train in Las Vegas was a legitimate coincidence. That, or she'd identified the weak link in his circle.

Pushing up on Othello, Ciera could potentially get closer to Joaquin. But did she know how messy things got when you tried to use a user?

"Ciera's life is in Florida, Othello. Whatever it is you're offering her, take it off the table."

"That won't work for me."

"Every woman you touch, you destroy. Give a shit, just once."

"Like Ciera was ever special to you?"

Joaquin felt anger shudder along his vocal cords as he spoke. "She lost candidacy for 'special' when she poked holes in my condoms with a sewing needle." But Othello had already known that she'd attempted to unsafe-sex her way to a pregnancy and a payday, because Joaquin had told his cousins why he'd put her on foot patrol.

Joaquin set his glass on the bar, observing Othello with hard, narrowed eyes. "I've had enough of this drink. Want it, too?"

Othello flipped up his middle finger. "The drink, the woman—keep them. I don't need your sloppy seconds."

Muttering a sarcastic "Ho, ho, ho," Joaquin deserted the bar.

The situation could have been defused, had he been in a take-the-high-road sort of mood. But his cousin's no-consequences, no-responsibilities attitude needed some tweaks. Let him cool his temper in a limo or dabble with table games in the casino. Maybe he'd realize that sleeping with his cousin's conniving ex was one too many degrees of disturbing.

Making tracks for the exit, he raked his hands down his face, then cursed.

A streak of brown makeup smeared one palm. In his haste to get the hell on with his day, he'd forgotten to have the makeup artists undo whatever they'd done to cover up the scar on his cheek.

He scrubbed the area ruthlessly with the back of his hand, using the other to frisk himself for a cloth. Keys. Wallet. Phone.

"Mother—"

"Before you drop the MF-bomb, why don't you ask me if I can help with…whatever it is you're doing?" All confidence and bubbliness with a little haughtiness sprinkled on top, Martha observed him from a few feet away. The lobby's lion statue sat regal beside her.

Both were probably mocking him.

And he almost smiled at the thought.

Without invitation, she glided closer. "This place is infested with media. Just an FYI."

"Not necessary. I brought them, in a way. Taped interview, all the fun stuff." He flashed his makeup-smudged palm. "Got tissues? I need to de-goo my jaw."

"It's called *concealer*, Joaquin. Not goo. And I have something more effective than tissues. Makeup remover." She grinned, patting her purse. Wearing a short dress so silky it resembled pale pink liquid, she almost sucked him in completely with that luminous smile. "Come with me, champ. I'll 'de-goo' you, and won't even ask you to buy me dinner first."

Joaquin's brain tripped, but somehow he heeded her instructions to meet her at the absolute last place the press might search for him: a wedding chapel.

"I got seasick a lot when I was a kid," Martha said softly, when he met her in front of the Cherish Chapel. "I was actually afraid of boats. Just getting close to one triggered this compulsion to puke my guts out. The look on your face right now is the *exact* look I used to have whenever I stepped on a boat."

"I generally avoid weddings unless for some misguided reason a friend or relative sticks me on the guest list."

Martha looped her arm around his, and her sugary perfume began seducing his common sense to oblivion. "My parents are fans of the aggressive approach. To cure my fear and seasickness, they put me on dozens of boats. Yachts, canoes, glass-bottom boats, so on and so on."

Damn. At night did they tuck her into bed with stories of sunken ships? "And you puked until your body could puke no more?"

She grunted a sexy chuckle. "Not quite. The gist of this is I'm sea-healthy nowadays. So I prescribe that you attend dozens of weddings. Church weddings, beach weddings, Wiccan weddings, so on and so on." She started walking and he moved with her, disturbingly satisfied to be so close to her again. "I'm inviting you to my wedding. Call me misguided."

"You're not getting married."

"Someday." Untangling their arms, she whispered, "A human Muscle Milk ad with a high and tight is tracking us."

Joaquin gave the security specialist a discreet nod. "It's what he's paid to do," he murmured to Martha.

"Oh. Of course. I get it." This time the smile she offered was a touch wistful. "What kind of prince would you be without royal guards?"

When they reached their destination, she announced, "Groom's dressing suite."

"That's got to be locked."

"Precisely why I rented it for my own salacious purposes while you were finding your way around this ginormous place." She tugged the key card from her purse. "The Blue name opens doors in this town—literally. I'd prefer if your royal guard stayed out here…"

Joaquin signaled the man to venture no farther, then joined Martha in the suite's stylish dressing room.

"I got so caught up in figuring out how to get this paint off my face that I forgot to ask what you're doing here in the middle of a workday," he said, hanging back and watching her take in the accommodations. Yeah, he really could spend hours admiring her ass.

"Slayers damage control. And I don't think I ought to say more. You might be a...*Dolphins fan*."

"Observer. I don't have NFL allegiances."

"You have an allegiance to my family, don't you?"

"In business and friendship, yes. As far as entertainment goes, if the Dolphins offer a better game than the Slayers, I'm watching the Dolphins."

Martha nodded. "Honesty's not always cute, but it's valuable."

"Glad you think so. And leaking NFL dirt isn't my priority when I've got twelve rounds coming in a month."

"Okay, I'll share. The media's already picked up the scent." She unzipped her purse and started to root around inside. "One of our players had a play-offs-euphoria-induced transgression. Anyway, his *transgression* was captured on cam and uploaded on YouTube last night."

"Get the video taken down."

"Obviously we've gone that route. But I still spent my morning brainstorming press statements and social networking responses with my colleagues and his publicists. The video had racked up over a hundred thousand hits by dawn."

"A hundred *thousand*? Shit. Was he recorded getting a lap dance?" The reference to their run-in at Mandalay Bay had one side of his mouth quirking up.

"Correct—almost." Martha held up a package of makeup remover wipes. "He was *giving* lap dances. As he claims, he and some buddies walked into a club during a bachelorette party and ended up dancing for liquor."

She brought the wipes into the restroom and waited while he washed away the concealer residue on his hands. "Anyway," she said, reaching up with a wipe and stroking down the line of his jaw, "the video's tamer than I'd expected, but his fans like his good-boy image. Preserving it is what's best for his marketability and our team."

"Marshall and Tem don't want more scandal." Which would've been great for him to remember *before* he'd put his hand in her pants at the gym.

Martha tossed the first wipe into the trash and grabbed another. "Speaking of scandals, what might Mister Muscle Milk suspect is going on in here?"

"You're sexing me."

Martha gave him a skeptical frown. "Because a groom's dressing suite is the ideal location for a midday fix." She tossed the other wipe and selected a fluffy rolled hand towel to pat against his cheek. "Tell him I was gentle," she said as she left the restroom.

Joaquin turned to examine the results in the mirror. The scar had reemerged, and he was now a bit closer to comfortable. All he needed were some sweats and a gym.

Or, more than that, another taste of Martha.

He'd watched her face, worshipped her lips, the entire time she worked. That sweet-smelling perfume and that deliciously plump mouth made him feel like a moneyless kid in a candy store.

"Back to your normal beastly self?" she asked when he met her in the dressing room.

"Getting there."

"I hope the tie didn't suffer too much when you killed it." She came over to lift the two dangling ends. "You're upset today. Am I the reason? I mean, my goals haven't changed. Yours haven't, either. So we should be okay."

No. It wasn't okay that he couldn't stop wanting more. It wasn't okay that there was something about her that he needed.

"You didn't piss me off." That, he could say without lying.

"What or who did?"

"And. What *and* who." Joaquin removed the tie and jammed it into a jacket pocket. "My weight lifting was interrupted for an interview, and I found out Othello's sleeping with my ex."

"India?"

"Ciera, who pokes holes in condoms in hopes of becoming *accidentally* pregnant and entitled to *accidental* child support."

"What if she genuinely wants to be a mother?"

"If a baby's all Ciera's after, there are men out there who actually want to be fathers. That's not me—and it's not Othello, either."

Martha nodded. "Can't help with the Othello-sleeping-with-Ciera dilemma, but I *can* help with the weight lifting." She propped her fists on her hips. "Lift me."

"What?"

"I'm a certified fairy-tale aficionado. I want to be swept off my feet."

The suggestion was ridiculous, ludicrous—

Ah, hell. Joaquin took a step, knelt and scooped her up high. He lowered her, then lifted even higher. Again. Again.

She gasped, hair bobbing, legs swinging. "Careful! Precious cargo."

He knew. Damn, did he know. "Had enough horseplay?"

But the moment he set her loose, she put up her hands, palms out. "I like to be swept off my feet, but I'm sturdy when I need to be. Strike."

The silliness of the moment darkened. "No, Martha."

"Why not? Fighting's your perfection."

"I won't take a swing at you, not even for play. I'd never, *never* hit you."

"What if I hit you first?"

"Then I must've really deserved it. But I'm trained to take hits and keep going."

"That 'hard-hearted machine' logic again?"

"Point is, this hard-hearted machine won't strike you."

"Unless you're angry enough?"

Joaquin went completely still. His temper had been tested too many times to count, but not once had he roughed up a woman. "If you have to ask that question, maybe you should walk. Now. Because you shouldn't be with anyone who makes you feel unsafe, and if that includes me, I can accept that."

Aggression was the fuel for his sport. Outside the ring, it could be damning. It was what turned some women off boxers and mixed martial artists. It was what his ex-fiancée had blamed as the cause of pain and suffering in her attempt at a civil suit against him for punitive damages in the wake of losing custody of her baby. Fear, she'd claimed, had motivated her to cheat with the man who'd once been Joaquin's real estate agent and friend.

Martha dropped her hands. "Boxing's violent. And the risks you take scare me," she said unashamedly. "But I've never felt unsafe with you. Am I being misguided now?"

"At the gym the other night, you told me to do what's right for me," he said. "I will if you will."

"Okay." Pale pink silk and sugary perfume swamped his senses when Martha eviscerated the distance between them. Opening his suit jacket, she said, "Your royal guard thinks I'm sexing you up. Wouldn't want to mislead him."

One taste. That's all he would need to get him through to…when? To the day he moved along to someone who wasn't his mentor's daughter and who didn't buy into a fairy tale he wasn't equipped to deliver? To next month when he was fresh from his fight at the Garden Arena? To the next time he could have Martha alone like this and taste her again?

Sliding the jacket down his arms, she stretched upward

and he saw the flirty glint in her dark eyes dim with concern. "I don't think I should want this, but I can't not touch you every chance I get."

Oh, God, this was how he needed her. Honest. Raw. Unscripted. Moist lips and warm skin and hungry hands.

When his arms sprang free of the jacket, he caught her waist and took her with him to the plush chair that rocked back on two legs at the force of their weight. It righted with a firm slam that shook them both.

Surprised, Martha laughed as she straddled his thighs. "That was exhilarating."

Joaquin pulled the straps of her dress over her shoulders and down until he uncovered her bra.

"Mmm, searching for something in particular?" she murmured as his hands cupped her.

"Your piercing." But he was after more than that. Though he shouldn't be, he was desperate for her, as though she was a damn necessity.

Unhooking the bra, he peeled the garment off and closed his mouth over the tip of one breast, then the other.

A hand over her mouth, Martha stifled a moan that he felt pulse through him.

"Give me your mouth, Martha." He urged her closer, kissing her hard.

"Take it. Take more." She clutched his hand and brought it down to her ass. "Keep taking until you're reminded that you're still a man, not a hard-hearted machine."

But a knock on the door had her springing up in an instant.

"Sir?" the security specialist who'd trailed them called through the door. "Is everything all right?"

"Yes. We're—"

"Leaving," Martha cut in, from the corner of the room where she'd escaped to, looking like a sexy wood nymph with her skin flushed and breasts exposed.

"Okay," the specialist said, then all was quiet for a good, agonizing five seconds.

"We're crazy," she announced. "We have to be. This is trouble."

"So we stop here? Don't ever take things as far as they went that night four years ago? Or even as far as they went the other night?"

"That would be the noncrazy choice." Martha ditched the corner to snatch her bra from the floor.

"All right." He should've kissed her longer, held her tighter. "But seeing you with your lipstick messed up, your beautiful tits wet from my mouth, your body shivering for me? *That* reminds me that I'm a man, not a machine."

Confusion flooded her eyes. She put on the bra, straightened her dress. "So we're done." Another sharp, conflicted glance. "Aren't we?"

He had to say it—and believe it. Holiday miracles and happy endings weren't in their future, because those things were meant for better men. Martha was meant for a better man. "We're done."

But he walked away troubled with the sense that they were both liars.

Chapter 8

When Martha went to bed on Christmas Eve, visions of sugarplums weren't dancing in her head. Dangerous impulses were.

She blamed it on the European necktie she'd successfully laundered herself—thanks to an internet tutorial— and had had professionally gift wrapped at a high-end specialty boutique.

Okay, perhaps on the surface it wasn't usually good taste to pass off a person's own possessions as Christmas presents. But gifting Joaquin the tie that had tumbled from his jacket pocket during her mission to sex him up good and proper at MGM Grand? And including a note that read "I resuscitated your necktie"? Well, it would be more of an inside joke, a way to shrug and airily say "No regrets."

Yesterday she'd been struck with the wicked inspiration to do so during her parents' party. While a fleet of award-winning designers transformed Marshall and Tem's main floor into a spectacular Christmas wonderland, she'd helped Tem's assistant with the guest list and had spotted Joaquin's name with the word *confirmed* beside it.

At least she'd taken the care to clean the tie—and she'd done so without ruining the fabric. That in and of itself was a gift.

Anyway, what to give a man who was more naughty than nice and had practically anything he could want in the free world?

A reason to laugh the kind of laugh that baited the dimple in his cheek and teased her like a million little kisses. Could a necktie and a sarcastic note accomplish that? Setting the gift at the foot of the bed and snuggling under the covers, she'd hoped so.

But now, at six can-I-go-back-to-bed o'clock, with Christmas being ushered in on gray skies and her mood preset to crappy, she was having reservations.

What if he didn't find the joke funny? What if someone at the party asked him about the tie? Worse—what if he brought a date and *she* asked about it?

As far as solutions went, primping and driving to Ryder's Boxing Club at an early hour was the most reasonable, even if the most inconvenient. There were perks, though: pit-stopping for fresh bakery doughnuts and leaving the tomb-like quiet of her house behind.

Sure, she'd appreciated the silence of the house when she'd taken ownership last month. It had been a perfect environment for studying, and would be again once the next term began.

But if the place was going to be her home, it needed more noise, disorder and character. Waking up to a completely silent Christmas morning, with no family or friends within reach, had introduced her to loneliness. And she despised it.

So she gladly traded a few laidback do-nothing hours for a place rich with noise, disorder and character.

The gym was unlocked and, expecting to find Joaquin all sweaty and focused and sexy, she added a little pizzazz to her strut. Which was for no practical reason, because they'd chosen the "un-crazy" route that prohibited getting hot and horny together.

No one stood in the ring or milled around the weight-training stations. Muffled voices came from the rear of the building.

Drawn to the bulletin board, to the flyer advertising the Ryder vs. Brazda event, she waited. It was the same image that had begun appearing on billboards in November. People had started to predict a winner before the matchup had even been officially announced. Once the fighters had greeted the media, the hype had grown exponentially.

Eliáš Brazda was a dangerous boxer, determined to usurp the power of Las Vegas's prince.

Joaquin Ryder was a living legend. America's rags-to-riches champ, a man who could retire at any moment and enjoy the prime of his life at the precipice of unlimited luxury. But he called himself a beast, defined himself as something engineered for fighting...for violence.

She'd seen him box before. She'd watched his strength mercilessly immobilize warrior-like men and his fists damage without relenting. She had seen him fight as if victory was oxygen.

Martha knew that *undefeated* only applied to boxing. Outside the ring, he could be humbled and hurt, capable of honor, respect, compassion.

Quit, Martha. A man laughs at a stupid joke and gives you an orgasm, and suddenly you know him completely?

Giving herself a mental kick, she turned away from the board. Carelessness was letting attraction shake loose everything she'd already decided about sex and love and her future.

Joaquin might satisfy her kink for rough-around-the-edges men, but incompatible couples didn't usually find their way into fairy tales. He was ten years older, lived across the country, didn't want children and beat the crap out of fighters for a living. The violence of him alone should've sent her running. Instead she was at a gym on Christmas morning with doughnuts and the necktie he'd left behind after groping her in a dressing suite.

Martha stood stationary as Joaquin's uncle and a lean, hard-faced man trudged in through an entrance at the rear of the building.

Jules Ryder preceded the other man, who carried what

looked like a child-size backpack, which he jerked out of reach when Jules made a grab for it.

The men disappeared into an office, and she heard more muffled conversation.

Where was Joaquin?

She started to approach the office, but the door swung open and the stranger strode out, sans backpack. Staring after him, puzzled, she didn't see Jules materialize in the doorway.

"Ordinarily I welcome beautiful ladies who bring me— what's that, doughnuts?—but the gym's closed," he said, advancing quickly.

"Who was—"

"Repairman. Washer's gone to hell."

"Got the feeling he'll be back soon."

Jules held her gaze, as though trying to read her thoughts. "What's that supposed to mean?"

"He left without his toolbox." Or his backpack, now that she thought about it.

"I'd hate to lug around a stocked toolbox just to give estimates, too," he said with a liberal amount of agitation. "No labor on Christmas."

"Didn't mean to offend." She was taken aback at his tone and the taut tension clearly visible in the way he shifted from foot to foot and flexed his fingers. "I have something for your nephew—"

"Doughnuts?"

"No. A gift."

"Joaquin's not coming in. Tor and Othello took him to Reno last night. A man trains hard, he needs to get the edge off."

Edge?

Martha almost dropped the doughnuts. The suggestion made her entire anatomy sting, and damn it, that really pissed her off.

I'm not supposed to care. We agreed to be done. So he's

*free to sample Reno women and I'm free to eat this whole
box of doughnuts.*

Except for the doughnuts-bingeing part, it was sound
reasoning. After all, she was standing in Ryder's Boxing
Club now to return his tie and get on with her professional
life, her sex life…the life she had *before* he'd crashed into
it again and twisted her inside out with mind-blowing foreplay.

"They'll be back in Vegas in time for your folks' get-
together," he said.

Get-together. Martha could almost see the disapproval
that'd saturate her mother's face if she were to hear that.

"Is that the gift? I'll put it in my office." Jules was already prying it and the box of doughnuts from her grip.

"Don't trouble yourself," she protested.

"No one goes into my office if I'm not there, if you're
worried about it disappearing," he assured. "Give it."

Jules carried the items to the office, then the door
slammed shut. Martha was on her way to knock and demand the gift back—she could write the doughnuts off as
a lost cause and have an excuse for a gourmet breakfast on
the Strip—when her phone erupted in a rap song.

"Merry Christmas," she greeted her sister Charlotte.

"Martha, I'm at your house, but you're not."

And here Martha had assumed the early-morning pop-in
was their mother's signature move. "I'm at the Ryders' gym."

Charlotte paused. "Doing what?"

Having the weirdest ever encounter with Jules. "Delivering doughnuts, but the boys all went to Reno to play."

"I need you back here."

Only something drop-everything serious could strip
Charlotte's voice of its confident strength.

"Okay," Martha said, jerking around to head for the exit.

Driving as fast as she could without winding up with a
Christmas speeding ticket, she returned home to find Nate
Franco's ride behind her gates.

She rushed into the house. If her instincts were wrong and this *was* a let's-check-up-on-Martha ambush—and Charlotte had recruited her man to assist—she was going to change her locks.

"Guys," she said, joining the pair in the living room. "What's up?"

Charlotte pushed off the sofa. "It's about Nate's father."

Oh, goody. The man who'd sold the Las Vegas Slayers to the Blues and then accused Marshall of acquiring the franchise by force. His lies had only led to the actual truth—that he'd been involved in an illegal gambling network and had bribed coaches and players to manipulate games. "Not to offend," she said to Nate, who sat with his fingers steepled and his handsome face dappled with fury, "but your father isn't someone I want to concern myself with."

"Afraid that's not an option right now," he said. "My brother found out Dad's attorneys are issuing a statement to the feds and the NFL that says Marshall was a coconspirator in the misconduct prior to being approved to buy the team."

"Bullshit." Martha looked to her sister. "Clearly it's another lie."

"I know. Nate knows—"

"So why are we wasting Christmas morning on this ridiculousness?"

"We need a game plan in place before the media gets wind of it. Ma and Pop are probably on a call with the GM or their lawyers. We need you and the PR team to get ahead of the media on this one."

Approaching the play-offs, their men didn't need a distraction and the franchise didn't need to be engulfed in this kind of hell.

Charlotte bowed her head, and pushed her fingers through her mane of curly hair. "Uh, look, Martha…the angle Al Franco's going with claims Pop showed interest in buying three seasons ago."

Three seasons ago, the Slayers' record had sunk. The team had become the joke of the league and hadn't shown signs of resurrection until the Blues had taken ownership.

So what did that mean for Alessandro Franco's scramble to bring the Blues down with him?

Ah. "Marshall Blue shows interest in the team two years before he acquires it. Because buying a winning team isn't as marketable as buying the crappiest team in the league and taking it to practically perfection," Martha said, visualizing how the situation could be interpreted. "To lay the groundwork, he gets Al Franco onboard to bring that record down, down, down and keep it at the bottom beyond one season—'cause only one losing season could look like a fluke and not hold the media's attention."

"Then," Charlotte said, "Marshall brings his wife on as co-owner, employs his daughters, and he's making a statement about gender equality in football. The franchise has its most stellar season, and Marshall looks like the man with the golden touch."

Frustrated, Martha sank into a chair. "Except Al Franco is a liar. Pop *and* Ma bought the team because they were willing to put in the work to make it successful in ways Franco never achieved."

Again she eyed Nate. She almost wanted to hold him accountable, because he was accessible and she was desperate to do something that didn't make her feel defenseless. But he was here now because his loyalty was to her sister, her family. "My feelings wouldn't be hurt if you left. I wouldn't want to sit silently while people tore down my father."

"When a man's wrong, he's wrong," Nate said, but he pushed to his feet. "I need to drive out to Henderson, talk to my brother—"

"Go," Charlotte agreed. "I'll get a driver to swing by if sis can't give me a lift."

Nate started for the foyer, but Charlotte said his name

once, then sprinted to him. Colliding, he gripped her, locked her in his arms and in his kiss.

It knocked the wind out of Martha's sails, damn near sank her ship in guilt. Nate wasn't a strictly by-the-book man. He'd manipulated and deceived and done things he said he regretted, but he hadn't inherited his father's maliciousness.

Al Franco's actions wouldn't take a toll on just the Blues and their football team, but also Nate and Charlotte's relationship.

"I didn't fall in love with you because I take the easy route," Charlotte said to Nate.

"Good." He squeezed her booty and let her go. "Don't ever say I'm easy. You'll scandalize my rep."

Charlotte laughed at the irony, and Martha wanted to, also.

Except jealousy choked her. Would *she* ever feel secure in the resilience that came with love? Would *she* ever know the rewards that came with trusting her risky heart, even when it wanted a man who wasn't storybook perfect?

Or would she keep the habit Chelle had described: boot men out of her life all day long, then dream about fairy tales at night?

After walking Nate out, Charlotte returned to the living room sofa. "I— Damn it, never mind."

"Lottie?"

"Before we take action, let's forget that Marshall and Tem are our parents. Who are they?"

"A mega-successful husband and wife. A man and woman who mastered the skill of getting what they want."

"Mastered it how?"

"Fundamental stuff. Perseverance, sacrifice, risks, tough choices. Charlotte, this is all leading to what?"

"Their methods *can* be Machiavellian. Ask Danica. Ask yourself, Martha. They demand family loyalty, but it's the business that they put first."

"Completely true, and that might seem two kinds of screwed up, but it's also how I know Marshall and Tem—Pop and Ma—didn't do what Al Franco is claiming." She plunked down on the sofa, nudging her sister playfully. "Move. I prefer this cushion."

"Too bad. Guests get first dibs." Charlotte sighed. "Hey. How do you know?"

"Protecting the business is the utmost priority. Making a dirty deal to buy it would mean that they'd jeopardized it from day one."

"God, that was a lucid defense." Charlotte seemed impressed—no, stunned.

"I have experience beyond men and mixed drinks."

"You're a purveyor of sarcastic one-liners."

Martha tipped an imaginary hat.

"Anyway, I didn't want to doubt or misunderstand our parents. But Nate's father also demanded loyalty, and what'd he do? Betray. He's a corrupt man."

"To put it mildly." A man who'd not only gamble on his team but would pay a player to injure his son wasn't deserving of an adjective as pleasant as *corrupt*.

"Nate didn't think that side of his father existed. Danica didn't think our parents could manipulate her as they had when she was GM. That's all I'm pointing out."

"What's her take on the situation?"

"I'll tell you when I find out. Called her and Dex, left messages. Guess they're busy."

"Busy getting their holiday delight on?" Martha wise-cracked. "On that note, would y'all please stop ambushing me? I'm going to start confiscating keys."

"Who did it first?"

"Ma. She thought my friend Gideon and I were having sexy times, because my pants were off and—" She stopped at her sister's wide-eyed look. "Anyway, she was wrong, I told her so and we fought about Christmas decorations."

"Oh. I thought the mantel-only decor was a trend I'd missed."

"The mantel would be bare, too, if Joaquin hadn't helped." Martha got up and touched the *H* stocking holder.

"Nice."

"Yeah."

Their time together *had* been nice. But short-lived. Now he was in Reno and she was in Las Vegas mooning over a man who wasn't good for her. "And I don't even have doughnuts."

"Doughnuts?" Charlotte asked.

Oops. "Just thinking about breakfast."

"You brought doughnuts to the gym but didn't eat any?"

"Jules swiped all twelve of them. Joaquin wasn't there, anyway. Okay, *what* are you laughing at?"

"Don't know why," her sister said between giggles, "but this reminds me of something you did when you were... seven? No, eight, because it was my graduation party."

What would Christmas be without an embarrassing remember-when story?

"It was a scorcher. You piled five scoops of ice cream on one freaking cone and searched the entire estate for Joaquin because you wanted to give it to him yourself."

The ice cream had dripped everywhere and she'd been sentenced to the indoors for the rest of the day. It'd been mortifying and not funny in any shape or fashion.

"It was adorable, the crush you had on..." Charlotte's laughter died. "Oh, Martha. Not him."

"Isn't that what people told you? 'Oh, Charlotte. Not Nate Franco.' Or what about 'Oh, Danica. Not Dex Harper.'"

"Are y'all hooking up?"

"Wow, because bringing a man doughnuts is a certain sign of sex delirium?"

"Are you having sex with him?"

"No." *Not at this very moment.* "If I were, what difference would it make? You and Nate can joke about scandalized reputations, but critics don't say about you what they say about me. So what's one more man?"

But Joaquin Ryder wasn't just one more. He was someone she'd known most of her life. He was someone she'd hurt, who'd hurt her in return. He was a man who made her feel safe and beautiful.

As her mother had said, if something could make her feel beautiful, Martha should make it hers.

Problem was, they'd both chosen to back away.

"Get over the crush, before he notices," Charlotte said gently. "Don't complicate things. Don't be the girl trying to catch his attention with sweets."

"Okay," she said, because that was easier than the truth. "Want to get something to eat?"

"I was about to attack the wax fruit." Charlotte pointed at the bowl on the coffee table. "I'd love to get something."

"Waffles, please. And if you're going to cook eggs, I take 'em scrambled."

"Your house, your food, your creations."

"I could cook, but that means you'll have to eat it. Or the wax fruit."

No hesitation. "Where do you keep the skillets?"

Martha skipped ahead of her to the kitchen. "Thought so!"

"Brat."

"Merry Christmas to you, too."

Tonight was the night to bring out the new toy. Putting his Hennessey Venom GT on the road would be Joaquin's way of celebrating Christmas. No clubs, no strippers, no repeat of how he'd spent last night in Reno.

Othello's idea to turn the city out had been his attempt at apologizing for hooking up with Ciera Byron. But liquor, luxury and ladies hadn't made up for a damn thing when Othello had been too preoccupied getting VIP'd by strippers to actually say sorry.

Tor had left his wife at home, but had returned to Vegas with her name in permanent calligraphy on his biceps. Joaquin imagined it'd be New Year's before she let him back in her bed.

As for Joaquin, he had no apologies, but had last night been a match of Ryder versus Reno, he'd have taken a loss. That it had been a hundred-thousand-dollar night didn't nick him. He'd eaten, gotten massaged, been entertained on a superficial level. There'd been fans on the street and hecklers in his path, cameras in his face and women's whispers in his ears.

There had been pressure. He thrived under pressure. But this morning he'd craved Vegas and left Reno hours ahead of his hungover cousins.

He'd wanted a break from the lifestyle of Joaquin Sinner Ryder, Las Vegas's prince.

Who decided to call him that anyway?

No one rode in the Venom with him, only one security vehicle followed and he felt all right. At least, better than he had trapped in a flashy-ass motorcade in downtown Reno.

Dressed in a Burberry tux, with a bottle of Perrier Jouet and a two-foot-tall peppermint candy cane—an impulse gift he'd bought for Martha—beside him, he drove.

A formal Christmas dinner was something he'd never experienced as an adult. Depending on his calendar, he could be found training or nightclubbing. Childhood memories showed him images of the Ryders gathered around a table passing trays of turkey slices and biscuits and bowls of potatoes.

Knowing that anything the Blues hosted was drenched in class and extravagance, he'd anticipated a decent turnout.

Not a solid hundred automobiles—and more coming—angled with precision along both sides of the private street. The massive estate, beaded with lights, looked as though the sky had opened up and rained glimmering white gold.

The brightness blazed over the street and touched the swaying waves in the lake.

Because the Venom was his 1.2-million-dollar new toy, Joaquin didn't want to share. He waited for his personal valet to emerge from the security car and take the Venom's keys, then he joined the flow of guests entering the house.

Rarely did tangibles do more than mildly amuse him anymore, but from the harp—paired with a diamond-gowned harpist—set up in the foyer, to the gold place cards in the dining room, to the ballet dancers performing in the ballroom, to the decked-out Christmas tree that looked like something Paul Bunyan could've felled, even Joaquin couldn't deny being impressed.

In the span of twenty-four hours he'd experience a hundred-thousand-dollar night in Reno and a million-dollar Christmas dinner...and all he cared about right now was giving Martha a candy cane.

"Shall I take those?" an usher offered.

Joaquin handed him the champagne bottle only and carefully perused the rooms. Political figures, athletes, TV celebrities, musicians, corporate somebodies. They knew his name, shook his hand, commented on his upcoming fight. But none of the faces he scanned belonged to the woman he searched for.

The peppermint was almost overpoweringly fragrant even through the cellophane. Or had anticipation heightened his senses?

Casting a glance at the wide spiral staircase that speared the center of the floor, he didn't see Martha among the people loitering on the stairs.

They'd drawn the boundary, and erasing it would make them liars. Yet he wanted a teasing look, a smart-mouthed remark. A reaction.

"Glad you could show, Ryder." Marshall Blue's large frame carved through a knot of guests. "I saw Jules and his boys come through 'bout a half hour ago. They're being taken care of."

"Appreciate it."

"Act like family, you get treated like family." Some referred to Marshall as a titan, but tonight vulnerability could be detected in the set of his deep, angry frown. "A word?"

Dread leaped through him for a second before he dismissed it. Marshall wouldn't have found out about Joaquin's *familiarity* with Martha's body and waited until Christmas night to off him. But then again, the Blues did everything in extreme style.

"A word about?"

"BC Group. My lawyers are in the study. What are you drinking?"

"Shots."

"Anything?"

"Yeah, surprise me. It's a holiday." As they walked, Joaquin tried to focus. What kind of conversation could he hold if he was preoccupied with getting another greedy look at the man's daughter?

A server waiting outside the study took the drink order and returned quickly with a vodka shot, which Joaquin knocked back before even settling into a leather chair in the mahogany-and-indigo room.

Marshall sat behind his desk. "Ryder, you enjoy a good story, right?" He addressed his lawyers. "Tell him the story."

As the men talked, Marshall retrieved antacids from a drawer and washed down a couple on a violent gulp of water.

Interpreting their legalese, Joaquin registered, "The Slayers' previous owner is after lighter consequences, thinks he can get them if he delivers Blue." He pointed his empty shot glass at Marshall. "You know investigators are going to call bullshit on Franco's talk, but that doesn't eliminate doubt."

"And doubt poisoning my army is the last thing I need," Marshall added, punctuating the statement with a savage swear. "Outside the NFL, there's a situation with Bio-Cures."

Joaquin listened to him explain that the energy company's execs and some shareholders had expressed reservations months ago in light of Alessandro Franco's initial allegations that Marshall had threatened bodily harm if not allowed to purchase the Las Vegas Slayers. Joaquin, who liked to stick to the shadows and keep an eye on his most lucrative corporate investment from comfortably afar, hadn't known the severity of the reservations.

Essentially, they would flex some corporate muscles to urge him to sell enough of his claim on publicly traded Bio-Cures to relinquish his status as the majority shareholder. Diminishing his presence in the company would strengthen their guard against his family's scandals.

"We suspect someone wants in—or wants more—and sees a potential opening should Marshall's investment be trimmed," one of the attorneys said.

"That ain't gonna happen." Marshall stood, rested his fists on the desk. "If or when Franco's statement leaks, BC Group is going to apply the pressure. I need your support—"

"Of course."

"—and I need you to be vocal. Involved. Out of the shadows. Consider it?"

Could he be relied on when it counted? Could he be more than the fighting machine, the bastard, he was born to be?

"I'll consider it."

The tall wooden door pushed open, and Marshall's already mean expression turned unrepentantly ugly. "Damn it, knock."

"Sorry, Pop."

Joaquin's heart staggered, bearing the impact when he saw Martha waltz into the study a few steps ahead of her mother.

Some women had butts, others had asses. Martha had an ass, and it shone under the metallic gold-green fabric that fondled her slender body as she moved.

She was all bronze and shimmer and curves and long limbs, scarcely contained in a gown held together by strands of jewels.

A meaningful, appreciative glance passed between the attorneys, and Joaquin eyed them coldly.

Martha arrived at the desk, set down a shopping bag. "Merry Christmas, Pop." She wiggled a sprig of something woven into her shiny, slicked hair.

Mistletoe. She'd tied mistletoe in her hair.

"Careful of my makeup," she warned, offering her cheek for a kiss. To the rest of them, she said, "Excuse me, fellas, but my father insists that I knock, so—" She rapped on his desk obnoxiously.

"All right. All right." Marshall's smile appeared painful, but it was genuine. "Go, men. Enjoy the party."

As the attorneys left, accepting drinks from the server waiting at his post, Joaquin approached Martha. She stood between her parents now, a treasure dangling out of his reach, a beauty out of his realm.

"Merry Christmas," Joaquin said to her, presenting the oversize candy cane.

At the exact moment she ventured forward, suddenly near enough to taste.

Grab her face, lick into her mouth. Pull her close, drink her moans.

Rather than do it and have Tem threaten castration or Marshall call him out for a street fight, he laid the cane in her hand and murmured against her hair, "So you won't steal mine the next time you're in my ride."

A snort of wry laughter or a smartass remark was expected. Not crystalline tears.

"I need to speak with my parents." Taking the candy,

she added in the silkiest whisper, "Tonight, if you want me, Joaquin, find me."

It was the sexiest proposition he'd ever heard, or the most baffling. Either way, he left the office dazed, hard and confused.

Chapter 9

Martha stared at the door as it closed, cutting off her view of Joaquin. Tonight he was temptation personified, and if her thoughts alone could determine which list Santa Claus put her on, then she'd just booked a standing reservation on *Naughty*.

As for the comic-prop-size candy cane he had for her, he should've given it to her with a kiss, as was customary should a woman go to the trouble of pinning mistletoe in her hair, and, ideally, when she wasn't flanked by her parents.

And after what Charlotte had said about Martha trying to catch his attention with sweets, she was burning to know if *he'd* search for *her* tonight.

Had whatever he'd done in Reno last night taken the edge off, as his uncle implied it would? Was the connection she felt really about nothing more than a man and a woman wound too tight and needing a lay?

"Martha," Tem said, stepping in front of her in glorious red-carpet worthy perfection, "are you all right? You seem upset."

Blinking, prying her stare off the closed door, Martha said, "Absolutely jolly. I'm at the most fabulous party in Vegas."

Approvingly, her mother smiled, then said to Marshall, "Our youngest says she has business advice, regarding the team."

And here we go with the patronization. "When we spoke

on the phone earlier, you said you'd keep this need-to-know and issue an internal statement if the guys start asking questions. I don't think that would be most effective."

"This decision doesn't affect your department, Martha," her father said, dismissing her. Taking Tem's hand, he started to walk toward the door.

"Marshall Blue, I'm a member of the Slayers unit, I have a voice and I want you to listen, damn it."

Goodbye, salary. Hello, severance pay. Now that she could foresee termination of employment, she instantly missed the stadium, her colleagues and even her fun-size office in S-Dubs.

"You, Martha, are a replaceable accessory to the Slayers unit," he said gravely. "Function in the role we gave you."

"So stay in my place?"

"Precisely." A swell of music, some familiar classic Christmas song that the band was playing in a rich R & B flavor, infiltrated the room, announcing that the ballroom was now open for dancing.

"I can't do that, sir, when you're too unfocused to see what's best for business."

Tem's gaze snapped to Martha. "You will not disrespect your father—"

"Sometimes, *Tem*, there has to be separation of business and family, even when the family's part of the business."

"Oh, there can be a separation. Starting with a note of gratitude for your contribution to the publicity department and termination of your employment based on your insubordination and flagrant disregard for our franchise's image." Tem yanked her hand from Marshall's grasp. "Then I can list the sacrifices we made to raise you—"

"No need," Martha said. "Your unadulterated disdain toward the daughter y'all didn't plan for isn't exactly a best-kept secret."

"It's not disdain. It could never be. What it is, Martha, is worry." Tem reached out as if to pat her cheek, but instead touched the mistletoe in her hair. "Wearing this, collecting kisses, makes you feel beautiful?"

"Unique. Playful. Funny. I could go on, but at some point it's just going to turn into boasting…"

"Antics like this—"

"Aren't crimes against propriety. So, if I'm not fired, I'd like to offer a business suggestion."

"One-woman mutiny," her father muttered, rolling his massive shoulders.

"Persistent, not mutinous," she countered. "I suggest that the team be made aware once we receive confirmation of what Nate claims his father is stating."

"And distract our men, send them into a damn panic going into divisionals?"

"No. It's to prepare them for media speculation and to get higher performance from each player."

Intrigued, Marshall crossed his arms. "*Higher* performance?"

"Yes, because this presents a test. It's motivation. How well each man responds to the noise in his ears will help us gauge his delivery and adaptability, as well as how much respect he has for our leadership and fidelity to our franchise." Martha hooked the candy cane on her wrist. "Ultimately, Al Franco's desperation will create a useful evaluation that can be to your advantage—if you choose to see it that way.

"Now, outside these doors are too many guests who haven't seen my mistletoe." Pointing at the bag on the desk, she added, "There's a gemstone globe inside. Pick a location, because I'm sending you on an after-play-offs couple's vacay."

"Oh," her mother said softly. "Martha…"

"Thought I'd try dipping into my trust fund for something other than beautiful things. And, underneath my antics and tendency to make you worry, I accept that your business and marriage come first."

"We took you to task, and a vacation gift still stands?" Marshall asked.

"The vacation's a vacation." Opening the door, she also opened the floodgates to a tidal wave of brilliant music. "The gift is *understanding*. Should you run out of gift ideas, that's on my wish list."

So was a Bugatti, but understanding mattered more.

By normal standards and definitions, Martha considered herself a sexual adventurer. Not quite an Indiana Jones, but she was inclined to experiment with the men she trusted and respected enough to engage in naked games.

But there were hard limits that included role-play that required safe words—because it only dragged her back to a bad night in New York when no words had made her safe—and PDB: public displays of banging.

Judging from what she'd narrowly escaped getting an eyeful of when she'd passed the third-floor loft of her parents' house and almost been struck with a red scallop Valentino pump, a pair of someones was indulging in frantic party sex.

Taking the spiral stairs fast, she'd almost dropped her candy cane and lost her balance, but arrived unharmed in the bustling gourmet kitchen, where only a handful of guests inelegantly devouring chips, sodas and store-bought cookies were in the catering staff's way.

"Schnapps?" asked her sister Charlotte's friend Joey, lifting a glass. Joey was a narc who'd been shot, rocked the hell out of a cane and owned a badass shoe collection. She was also the agent who'd blown the whistle on Al Franco's gambling ring and NFL misconduct.

"Pour!" Then Martha changed her mind. "Just give me yours. Keep the bottle."

Joey slid over her glass and turned up the bottle. "*Ay dios mio*. Over thirty, bumming Christmas dinner from my friends and drinking Schnapps straight from the bottle. Somebody call my mother, tell her she was right."

"Aren't you seeing someone?"

In answer, Joey turned up the bottle again. "Dish. I know you're packing gossip."

"Sort of. Someone was having sex in the third-floor loft."

"You saw ass?"

"No, but I know sex when I hear it." She pretended to fan herself with the candy cane. "And a red scallop Valentino almost beaned me on the head."

Joey twisted her mouth and checked her shoes. "I'm clear."

More guests squeezed around the counter for predinner junk food.

A prosecutor who'd become a national news celebrity during a highly publicized murder trial was delivering the punch line to a raunchy joke when Danica walked in.

"Because Christmas is the perfect time for a disturbing image like that," she said sarcastically over the laughter, rushing over to cover Martha's ears. "My innocent sister."

"I did give them a choice," the man said. "G-rated or X-rated. Unanimous vote for X."

Martha patted her sister's hands and told him, "The version I heard involved glitter, not Tabasco sauce."

"*Innocent*, right." With a wink for Martha, he hugged the woman beside him close. "The dance floor's calling our names."

"That's one big candy cane," Danica commented.

Martha tried to reach around it to set down her glass, but bumped it, propelling it off the counter.

She and Joey craned their necks to see it land on the floor in front of Danica's red scallop Valentino pumps.

Gasping, Martha knelt to grab the cane before her sister could. "Oh, my God."

"*You're* the loft-banger?" Joey snorted, then went back to seducing her Schnapps.

"The uh—um—"

"Sex at a party, Danni? A *family* party? Isn't sex the reason you and your man couldn't be reached this morning?" Martha picked up the peppermint carnage. Really, it had a few fractures and was still edible.

Danica sighed. "I'm sorry you saw—"

"And heard."

"—and heard what you did."

"If you were like this with your ex-husband, you hid it really, really well."

"Love's different for each person you're with. I was married for ten years and never loved that man this way. Dex and I, we want to be together every chance we get. It's passion you can't understand until you live it."

"On *that* note," Joey said, "I'm going to find out how many eligible men Tem put at my table."

As Martha had assisted with seating arrangements, she knew the answer was seven, but figured she'd let the woman make that discovery for herself.

"Aside from almost being bopped with a shoe, how's your Christmas?" Danica asked.

"I thought it'd be merrier than this."

"The mistletoe didn't garner enough kisses?"

She'd lost count of how many people had stopped for smooches, but she knew Joaquin hadn't been one of them. If he wanted her, he'd search for her.

"Martha, your candy cane needs a cast."

"It's broken." Metaphorically, it'd probably been broken from the beginning.

"It's salvageable. Just not perfect."

After a minister's prayer and a twenty-five-recipe dinner—Martha's favorite dish being steak au poivre—guests dispersed to roam with drinks in hand, mingle and gossip, and dance in the ballroom.

She fled to the staircase with her salvageable candy cane and a goblet of white chocolate mousse.

"Yo, brat." Charlotte, draped in a revealing black gown, waved. "Danica, she's on her perch, making assessments."

The naughty lady in red came rushing around the corner, and the two joined Martha on the staircase.

"You're not bored, are you?" Danica asked. "A bored Martha usually introduces a bad Martha."

Bad meaning a trending, scandal-attracting, trashed-in-the-tabloids Martha. At twenty-three, she wasn't burnt-out from the party-every-night lifestyle. But since she'd enrolled at UNLV's business school, she had begun to crave a life spiced with variety. Quiet and leisurely days in between nights of fast, loud parties.

"Lottie's the designated pretty-trinkets gift-giver, so I try to go for unexpected." Opening her silver clutch purse, Danica retrieved her smartphone and scrolled the photo album.

Bugatti, Bugatti, Bugatti...

When Danica held out the phone, Martha almost moussed the front of her dress.

Charlotte took the dish, and Martha was too stunned to demand it back.

It wasn't a Bugatti—or anything with four wheels. Instead, it had four itsy-bitsy paws and long ears and a fuzzy cottony tail. "A bunny?"

Explaining that her best friend, the daughter of a match-maker, had raved about rabbits' tranquility-boosting abilities, Danica said she'd enlisted her to find a rabbit that would be compatible with Martha's zodiac characteristics. "If you want someone to love and some companionship in that house…"

It wasn't the fairy tale, wasn't the exact way she wanted to bring companionship into her house, but she believed in ways that were intuitive more than logical that the rabbit belonged to her. "It's going to be Martha and Rabbit, Rabbit and Martha."

"Someone to love. Someone to love you," Charlotte said. "Want to come down to the ballroom? Ma and Pop are slow dancing. It's incredible to see."

Martha reclaimed her goblet, took a spoonful of mousse. "I *have* seen it, about every night for years. If there's anything they cherish above success, it's each other."

"Marshall and Tem…they've got secrets and hidden agendas, but don't we?" Danica turned to Charlotte, while Charlotte spied Martha, and Martha stared knowingly at Danica.

Were any of them ready to reveal?

Charlotte cleared her throat. "Nate and I should go. There're Christmas presents at his place with my name on them."

"And I," Danica said, "want to get out of this uncomfy dress."

Imagine how uncomfy you'd be if you'd actually kept it on all night?

Off they went, like ritzy mice scurrying to their hidey-holes.

"I found you."

Joaquin, in a tux with satin lapels that waited for her hands to caress slowly then grip with savage necessity, approached the staircase.

"And now that you have," she said, "what do you want to do?"

"Unravel you." One stair closer. Another. "Unleash you."

Any moment someone on a higher or lower level of the house could step onto the staircase, could see her arched back and his body almost, *almost* sheltering her.

It was terror and thrill intertwined, and she wondered if this was what Danica and Dex had felt, escaping to a loft in hungry, risky urgency.

"Give me a spot where no one else touched you tonight,"

Joaquin said in the softest yet harshest demand she'd ever heard. "Give me a spot to make mine."

Risk it. Make him be quick. Take what moments you can steal.

No. She couldn't do that. Because they needed to be alone. She needed him to take his time.

"I sat here in plain sight. The only way I could've been *more* in your face was if I'd wrapped myself in lights." She eased out of his shadow. "I made it too easy, but that's my habit, isn't it?"

"Where I come from, *easy* isn't the same as complicated and confusing. Every night since you climbed into my ring and let me touch you, I've been chained up in hell."

"Keep sweet-talking me like that and I'll fall in love," she said with an exaggerated eye roll. "Fact is, if something's too easy to claim, you don't respect it. You forget it. So, Joaquin Ryder, I'm not going to be your easy victory tonight."

You're going to be mine.

Escape was in the darkness. Joaquin's gated Promontory Ridge estate was set in shadows. No lights, no entourage, no delusions of celebration.

He'd left that behind at the Blues' place. All his house offered were a Christmas tree—trimmed but unlit—the scent of pine in the air and cranberry vodka.

Yeah, he thought, walking through the silence, shrugging off his tux jacket in one room, leaving behind shoes and socks in another, discarding his cuff links someplace else.

The blue LED flare of the wine refrigerator silently urged him to it. Grabbing a bottle of Smirnoff, he twisted the cap and drank.

Right now he wasn't Las Vegas's prince. Right now, he wasn't even a fighter.

Setting the bottle down, he shifted into his stance

and threw a tight jab into the darkness. He kept his chin dropped, extended his shoulder, put his weight into the offense. Speed and power were there, but it lacked grace.

Loosening his shoulders, popping bones throughout his skeleton, he tried again. Better, more disciplined, but short of perfect.

Failure.

Damn. Neither liquor nor the late hour could be blamed. In top form, he could spring out of a deep sleep and fight with immaculate brutality. In the rain, his technique was creative and his assault unstoppable. In a ring, with a championship on the line, he was undefeated.

Alone, with no opponents and no obstacles, he was flawed. Not a beast, but a man.

Because some part of him had stayed behind at Marshall and Tem's party: his concentration or his heart, he didn't know.

He *did* know who held his attention—and nothing about her was "easy." Tonight there hadn't been a place or time for them. Could be for the best, but his tense body disagreed viciously.

Joaquin carried the Smirnoff to the Christmas tree, crouched to plug in the lights.

The twinkling brightness soared twelve feet, illuminating the rock walls and dark furniture, but it didn't breach the blackness of his mood.

About to take to the stairs, he paused at the sound of his phone vibrating on the kitchen counter. Probably one of his cousins wanting to talk him into rolling out to an after-party somewhere.

Snatching up the phone to silence it, he got a look at the display. *Oh, shit.*

"I opened my gates for you," Martha said when he answered. "It's only fair for you to do the same for me."

Reciprocation? That's what she was after?

"Why are you here?" His voice echoed throughout the kitchen…or had frustration hollowed out his mind?

"I have a question."

If the gym was his territory, then his house was his sanctuary. Right now it was untouched, free of their knotted history and the hurt they'd inflicted on each other.

Maybe that's why he hated being here tonight. Maybe he needed that, the poison—or elixir—of their attraction.

He opened the door, sat at the base of the stairs and waited for the sugary fragrance he'd detected on her skin earlier.

She had smelled like the sweetest sin, looked like the most tempting dirty deed.

Easy? God, no. If things were easy, he wouldn't be wishing that he could give her what she needed—*be* what she needed.

Then there was sweetness, but it was only her perfume. Because there was anger and accusation in her stomp as she walked into his house, shut the door and searched until she spotted him.

"Why'd you give me this?" She dropped the beaten but still wrapped candy cane onto his lap.

"Um. It didn't look like that when I gave it to you," he said. "Did you break ice or kill a bug with it?"

"It fell off a counter." Her sigh was a whisper in his ears. "Why, Joaquin?"

"For a reaction. Even the tears." He picked up the peppermint cane, threw it an indeterminable distance and heard the faint sound of it skidding across the floor. Rising to his feet slowly, he watched her throat undulate as she swallowed.

"Tears that don't cross the waterline don't count." Superciliousness spiked her voice.

"Liar." Backward, he edged a few steps higher and she advanced, maintaining their proximity. How high up these stairs, how far into his home, how deep into his life would she go? "I caused them. They count."

"So it's 'get the edge off in Reno then entice Martha with candy canes and car rides'?"

"What edge?"

"Jules told me about Reno."

"You talked to my uncle?"

"At the gym this morning. We didn't say much. He wasn't acting like his normal Jules self. Sort of jumpy. He made off with a dozen doughnuts and the washer repair guy was over."

"TV guy."

"No, *washer*, according to him. Do you always have to be so contrary?" She scrunched her face. "Anyway, before you go after him, try to remember there *are* such things as Twitter and Google."

A man who wanted discretion wouldn't have ridden through Reno in a procession of limos, Hummers and pimp-mobiles, but that didn't matter. "You think I went to Reno and substituted you with another woman?"

"I think you *tried*."

"I didn't. I can't." One step higher, and she countered the move. "An edge? Nah, Martha. An edge wouldn't get in my head, touch my concentration. An edge wouldn't make me obsess about kissing you."

"Mistletoe gave you clearance."

"*Clearance?* No," he denied, solemnly shaking his head. "Not to do what I want."

Joaquin leaped down to where she stood. The limestone-walled staircase was wide and curved slightly in its tunnel-like ascent to the second floor. But sharing her step, her space, he knew he crowded her.

"You're holding me, know that?" He breathed in her scent, said her name on an exhale. Another night of teasing and tantalizing might end him. "You've got to release me."

"At the hotel we said—"

"We lied. We were wrong." He splayed his hand on the

limestone, scraping the pads of his fingers on the rough surface. "We didn't know."

Martha reached up, circled his wrist. "Want the kiss? Work for it." And pushing against his wrist, she loped down the stairs.

The sight of her swaying hips torched him. Joaquin didn't rush—he could take his time with her, and fully intended to. He knew exactly how he'd take that damn shimmery dress off…had plans for that mistletoe.

On the bottom step, she flirted with the jewel straps of her gown. Then he reached her, making contact this time, taking her hand and skimming his lips over her knuckles.

Biting her index finger, he groaned to hear her stunned little gasp.

Withdrawing, she told him, "I did give you a spot to kiss," and sauntered deeper into the house.

His feet touched the floor, and soundlessly he hunted. This time she *had* made things easy, because he could track her fragrance and the sound of her footsteps. Aside from that, she stopped in front of the glowing Christmas tree.

A present, for him.

"Show me," he coarsely demanded. "Show me what I can make mine."

Martha grabbed his neck, leaned into him and fitted her lips to his. "No one touched my mouth tonight, except you."

He swore against her soft, soft lips. Traced their shape with his fingers. Pushed the middle one into the wet heat of her mouth.

"Moan on it." He was reduced to whispers, his control weakening by the minute.

Boldly catching his gaze, she closed her lips and sucked.

"God." Martha Blue was going to break him. Damned if he wouldn't enjoy it.

A playful nip, then she let him slip free.

"This isn't going to be the perfect candles-and-flowers

night you'd wanted from me." He'd felt compelled to give her a choice, a chance to change her mind about this. About him.

"Candles and flowers don't make sex perfect. I've had great sex without 'em." A gentle smirk doubled the appeal of her beautiful mouth. "That bother you?"

"No. I've had great sex without candles and flowers, too."

A smirk doubled the appeal of her beautiful mouth as she toyed with her dress straps again. The jewels glittered under the tree's lights. "You know what I mean. Some men are fixated with what they have going on down there."

Unhooking his belt, he took her hands and laid them over his crotch. "And I'm satisfied with what I've got."

Firmly, she stroked him rigid. "So." *Again.* "Am." *Again.* "I." *Again.*

"Dress. Off."

Martha's hands lifted, and his rod leaped in protest. She turned, exposing a delicate zipper. Bringing down the zipper, he peeled back shimmery fabric to reveal smooth skin.

What had he done to deserve her—her lust…her trust?

Joaquin thumbed the straps over her shoulders, watched gravity lure the dress down her body to the floor in an inconsequential puddle of fabric.

She started to twist around, but he held her there, facing the tree. "Bra? Underwear? Not even a look, Joaquin?"

"I want what's underneath."

Quickly he found what lay underneath the metallic dress, scanty bra and open-in-the-ass panties: the only woman who could crack his guard by simply standing naked in front of him.

And another provocative surprise, when he gently turned her around again: a drop of platinum on her navel. A belly-button ring.

So this was her hidden piercing. Raking his fingertips over it, he said, "When I get inside you, when I make you come the first time, this is what I'm going to be looking at."

Martha yanked on his shirt, laying a kiss on each button before freeing it. "Give me as many rounds as you can last, Ryder."

Joaquin watched her sink to the floor after she worked the last button loose and stripped off his shirt. "A new boundary... We need one. Where do we stop? When?"

"Tomorrow," she said, and the regret that touched her eyes before she glanced down to unfasten his tuxedo pants told him she struggled with the one-word decision. "We take everything tonight."

One night. It didn't seem right that for all their history, all she meant to him, she'd end up a one-night stand.

But he had to accept, because— "I can't give you what you need, Martha. I can't be your fairy tale. I'm sorry."

"I don't want what I need for Christmas." Tugging down his underwear, she broke him down with a flick of her tongue. "I want what I *want*."

Chapter 10

Martha couldn't tell him the truth, that from where she was, on her knees with his calloused hands cradling her head and his gaze blazing into her, there was no distinction between *want* and *need*. They were halves of a whole, yet laying them together still didn't quite define the threads of thirst and possession weaving through her.

So what defined their connection?

Craving?

Appetite?

Obsession? He'd said that, confessed that he was obsessed with wanting to kiss her.

No other man had hooked her this way, but then she'd been told that love changed and customized itself.

She'd wanted to ban the word *love* from her heart, the way Joaquin had cut it from his vocabulary. Because love was the beautiful hell she'd plummeted into four years ago—when she'd been reckless and desperate and weak.

When he'd told her to get out of his life and take her love with her.

That love isn't this love...

It was different. It had to be. She'd changed, and so had he.

From thighs to shoulders, she caressed him as she stood. There were more scars on his body, more hardness to his face. More respect and fascination in his eyes when he watched her handle him.

This time she wasn't asking for something he couldn't

give, or wanting him to be someone he wasn't. Because he was right—he wasn't her fairy tale.

"What else is mine, Martha?"

Carefully slinking back, she watched him, watched desire wrestle restraint. The house was dead silent, the rush of her pulse in her ears deafening.

"Martha..." he said again, his voice riding a jagged groan. He closed in, his footsteps light, his body all power, threat and erotic persuasion.

"Show me." Joaquin wrecked her hairstyle to get to the mistletoe, then ran it lightly over her skin. The waxy texture of the leaves, the scratch of the tiny berries, brushed her mouth. Then her throat. Then her breasts. "Please, baby. Show me where you want my mouth."

Oh, my God. Had she dreamed this? Was it real that Joaquin Ryder, the Sinner, Las Vegas's prince, was *begging* her?

Martha took the sprig of mistletoe, twirled the skinny branch, and the leaves tickled her neck.

Then his mouth was on her, firm pressure and hot pleasure.

Breathlessly, she released a half moan, half scream. Well, he'd said he wanted to unravel and unleash her.

"And now where?" he asked.

"Get me to a bed first," she demanded. "A big, fluffy one. We're gonna be there awhile."

Cling. All Martha could do was hold on tight when Joaquin curled her into his arms and took off in a sprint. He moved too fast for her to register more than the cave-like stairwell he mounted two steps at a time and the shadows of the hallway he carried her through.

Master suite. Lair. Point of no turning back. That's where he stopped running, where he put her on her feet and let her move next.

Mistletoe in hand, she crossed to the larger-than-life bed.

It was all she cared about, the only feature she focused on besides the room's soaring windows.

"Can anyone see in here?"

"Maybe. If they really, really wanted to." He molded his hands to her ass. "What don't you want anyone to see?"

Martha heard the banter in his voice, and answered by yanking the top quilt off. She took a dive, landing in the middle of that luxurious marshmallow of a bed. "I don't want anyone to see me naked for you."

As daring as ever, she swept the mistletoe across her breasts. "Kiss me here."

Again, all she could do was cling, hold on, grip. Roughly, thoroughly, he sucked her flesh, adding a few stinging bites and soothing touches.

Coaxing him, massaging his scalp, she managed to slide the mistletoe down past her platinum navel ring. "Taste me here."

Four years ago he'd made her come with his mouth, but as he spread her thighs, exposed her and indulged, what had been a soul-shaking experience then now paled to a dim, muted memory.

Martha grabbed a pillow.

"What are you gonna do with that?"

"Bite it."

"Aw, hell, no." Chuckling, he stripped it from her hands and let it bounce off the mattress. "Want to bite something? Here I am. Or scream, 'cause that little moany scream you make drives me crazy."

"That dimple in your cheek drives *me* crazy." Rearing up, she kissed the indentation, grazed it with her tongue. "The stupid things I'd do to see this dimple."

Angling his head, pressing her deep into the mattress, he took her mouth without restraint. "Stay just like this. Need to get a condom." He furrowed his brow. "We *are* gonna be needing it this time, aren't we?"

Impishly, she shoved his shoulders. "Yeah, we're gonna need it. *Them.* Bring plenty, champ."

Returning to her, Joaquin sprinkled a fistful of condoms onto the sheets. Jokes and laughter abandoned her, and when he nudged himself into her, she closed her eyes. "Just take."

Bracing on one elbow, he reached for her. Their hands met in a collision of gentle and harsh, and their fingers laced. "I'm not going to screw you like a stranger. Like I don't care."

"What if asked you to?"

"Next round. Not the first."

A blend of passion and affection was what she'd wanted four Decembers ago, and what she was stunned to extract from Joaquin now. She was no virgin; her middle name was considered ironic.

But entwined fully with the man she loved, she felt... new.

An audience was waiting at Ryder's Boxing Club. Waking up semi-hard, Joaquin had reached for Martha. And found her side of the bed empty.

Her side. Things had gotten so twisted already that he missed her naked body beside him and her fragile whispers in the dark. He ached to rake her soft, springy hair back from her face, was pissed that sleep had cost him a few more hours with her.

Showering off the night and throwing on shorts, a cutoff shirt and sunglasses, he'd jogged downstairs and nearly sideswiped his housekeeper, who'd prepared him a protein shake. She arched a brow as she carted off last night's discarded clothes.

Then he'd stared at the Christmas tree, freakin' frozen as he replayed stripping Martha in front of it. What she'd done... The way she'd looked up at him...

Wound tight, he'd been primed for a brutal heavy-bag

workout. But he'd arrived too late to beat the crowd that usually started flooding in the moment the sign flipped to Open. Vehicles, motorcycles, bicycles—they filled the lot to capacity and lined up on both sides of the street. Inside were amateur boxers who belonged, a few trainers who wanted to jive around with Jules...and a crowd of people who wouldn't darken the door if not for the man with all the hype.

He'd come for a workout; they'd come armed with cameras and social media apps to see a show.

Jules, in his RBC sweatsuit, was in the ring, mitts on, with an amateur when Joaquin came into the gym.

Waving him off, intending to skip rope before getting his ringside gloves on, Joaquin went over to claim the bag he used on off days. Off days usually meant the days he didn't spar, but from the second he'd reached for the woman who'd probably bailed at the first sign of dawn, he'd felt wired with energy, but askew in the head. Thrown off.

Cheers and hollers erupted. People looking to make asses of themselves and get roughed-up on the way out the door tugged the ropes and booed the amateur—as if his training was some get-by entertainment until Joaquin arrived.

"Get loose," his uncle yelled, "then c'mon in."

"Nah," he said, crouching to get the rope from his gym bag. "No sparring."

"You keep learning, you stay undefeated," Jules shot back with authority. "Get loose, damn it, then let's go."

America's champ or not, Joaquin expected an almost daily earful of hell from his uncle in the weeks leading to an event. Jules Ryder wasn't afraid to cut his boys to size. From the day Joaquin had been rescued from a crack house and brought to live with Jules, he'd been lumped in with Tor and Othello—treated like a son.

Considering Joaquin was Jules's nephew *and* trainee, public chastisement was guaranteed.

Joaquin rattled off a few harsh swear words, the audience heckled and he got to work. Ten minutes of cardio had him coated in a light sweat and declining water and towels left and right.

Everyone wanted a connection—whether they got it standing close to him and snapping a goddamn selfie or by handing him a bottle of water and trying to bait him into a conversation.

Most days he obliged, accepted a water and posed for a picture. Today he wanted a gym where he could train, clear his head, get back to fighting perfection.

Taped and gloved, he faced Jules in the ring. The noise he could always tune out was a din.

"Shoulders too tight," cautioned Jules, who'd traded the mitts for gloves. "Keep your head moving. Stay fluid. Strong start's going to beat Brazda."

Joaquin exhaled hard, focused on his uncle from beneath the furrow of his brow and jabbed. Sparring, they engaged Jules's no-mercy routine, striking to injure, dodging knockouts, holding in the background the January matchup that'd decide his fate in this sport.

Throwing his right hand, he landed a jab, and was going into a left hook when his uncle threw an overhand right, connecting hard.

"Keep your position tight!" Jules swore, backing out of the line of Joaquin's assault. "Break. Break. Get in the office."

Ringside gloves off, Joaquin leaped out of the ring ahead of his uncle. Not wanting to stop moving—and finding no place to sit with clutter on the office chairs and a scatter of penny candy on the desk—he practiced footwork while Jules set up two amateurs to spar in the ring.

"You're gonna watch the tapes later," Jules said, striding in, his dark face drawn in a scowl.

"Taping today?"

"You need to see earlier footage, watch for the absence of the amateur shit you haven't thrown since high school." Jules got into his stance, mimicked Joaquin's left jab right hook. "Too easy to read, lax position, no damn chin coverage—how's that face feeling?"

"Cool." *Hurt like burning hell.*

"Your diet stable?"

"Yeah."

"Weight? Body fat? Last check you were perfect."

"Still am." His only perfection was physical.

"So what is this?" Jules grabbed for a handful of random fruit chews, dumped three in his mouth. "You hearing the noise?"

"Out there with the free neighborhood show?"

"The streets. Critics."

"Always do." But his emotional armor protected him from criticisms that he was too old, too predictable, too undeserving to live to fight another day.

Jules inhaled several more fruit chews. "Oh, yeah. Got a delivery yesterday." He shoved aside an empty doughnut box and surrendered something with fancy gift wrapping.

"No card. Who brought it?"

"Marshall's little girl. Martha."

Opening the box, Joaquin lifted a necktie from the satiny interior.

It was his, the tie he hadn't realized he'd left at MGM Grand.

Jules was holding a stark white card between his index and middle fingers. "Can't forget this."

I resuscitated your tie.

A grin hit his face, and aggravated the soreness from the jab his uncle had landed to his chin.

"Reno didn't do the trick?" Jules said around the knot of candy bulging in his cheek. "Any woman can do what Martha Blue's doing for you. That's a pair of panties you should've passed up."

Joaquin's fists went up before he'd realized he wasn't

outfitted in gloves and they weren't sparring. "Never, Uncle Jules. Never insult her."

Jules frowned as Joaquin relaxed his hands. "You're screwed if you want to bare-handed hit the man who put food in your mouth, dragged you out of juvie and kept you in this gym."

Jules went for another fistful of candy. "Filthy rich or dirt poor, a woman will break a man faster than anything else."

"Your wife—"

"Knew her place, and I could keep her out of my head when I needed to." Jules rubbed his forehead. "My sister was a woman, too. Go ahead, boy. Name *her* virtues."

"She was my mother." That was the start and end of her virtues. She hadn't been able to figure out who'd fathered her kid, and had raised him in a crack house where drugs, violence and raids were the norm, until she'd overdosed.

"Wives, mothers, sisters, daughters, aunts—family or friends, doesn't matter. They'll muck up stuff in a heartbeat." Jules shrugged. "Now, I like Martha, she's family. But she was born into money. You fought—literally fought—for it. Let her close and she'll start working on you."

"Working on me?"

"To get you out of the ring. You didn't let India or Ciera or any of the others break you in. Don't let Martha."

As effortless as it would've been to swing the conversation to Jules's son's recreational activities with Ciera, Joaquin accepted some hits full-on. This conversation was one of them. "Uncle Jules, with all due respect—"

"When people say 'with all due respect,' it damn near always means they've got something disrespectful to say. I don't want to hear that coming from you."

"Leave Martha out of the conversation."

"Leave it in your pants and I won't say another untoward thing about her. Or Marshall Blue can encourage you."

"Yeah, Uncle? You're going to involve him? Why? The. Fight. Is. Mine."

"What's outside the ring for you, Joaquin? Kids, a steady woman, a pet rock? Nothing. You're in *Sports Illustrated*, on commercials. You don't have a reason to *stop* fighting." Jules crossed his massive arms. "Ain't nothing wrong with that. Thing is, Martha's as high-maintenance as the rest of your women—probably more. If you're thinking she's something sacred… Son, she ain't a prude."

"I'm not, either."

"Okay. I'm trying to talk to you, man-to-man, and you wanna be funny." Jules pointed to the supersize Plexiglas rectangle that protected a poster advertising Joaquin's match against Brazda. "See that? Look at that machine. Nothing's behind those eyes, except fire."

Joaquin studied the poster. Deep creases on his face, cold fire in his narrowed eyes, his expression both arrogant and savage.

Machine. That's what he was. A man wouldn't defeat Eliáš Brazda next month.

A machine would.

Ca-ching! Bingo! Jackpot!

Avery bowed her arm into the donation bin at Faith House, as a fisherman would cast a net into water. Peering into the bin, she'd already identified her big bass.

She just hoped her arm was long enough to reel in the shoes. Seriously, who would toss a new-with-tags pair of clogs?

Only a few days had passed since the de-clutter staff Renata's son had hired had swiped over half of Avery's belongings, but she'd already become a pretty savvy donation-bin searcher.

Maybe she was stranded in Dummyville, population one, but she imagined if she looked carefully and exhaustively, she'd recover some of her stuff.

In the meantime, she had a replacement jacket and a pair of skinny jeans, thanks to a department store that had given her the items free of charge. And if she could reach just a *little* farther, she'd have a pair of designer clogs.

She hadn't asked Renata for real Christmas presents, had visited a church and prayed for her foster mom and had left without helping herself to refreshments, but she'd desperately wanted something for herself.

Desperately enough to snare the clogs, stuff them in her bag and hurry to the restroom.

She'd wanted to ask permission, but was afraid. Afraid someone would tell her the shoes had been donated by mistake. Afraid some of the other kids would laugh at her and she'd never feel comfortable showing up here again. Afraid her self-proclaimed nosy math geek tutor would get question diarrhea.

Even though she was planning to run away a good hundred bucks from now, Avery had signed up for Martha Blue's tutoring group anyway.

She supposed things could be worse than having someone fashionable and sophisticated and funny teach her mathematics.

She pushed to her tiptoes, extended her fingers…and caught the leather strap tying the pair together. Dumping the clogs into her bag, she dashed into the restroom. In the mirror, a girl who looked like a little kid but felt like an adult confronted her. She smoothed back her hair, then pulled it up. The loose curls flopped over her forehead. *Sophisticated?* Not even close. She needed to update her earrings, watch a few more YouTube natural hair styling tutorials, buy lip gloss.

After she slept. Ironically, she hadn't felt safe taking more than a few short, light naps since she'd changed her bedroom doorknob. He hadn't said anything, but Renata's son must be colossally pissed that she had changed anything— even something cosmetic—while the condo was for sale.

Avery glanced into her bag, suddenly swamped with guilt.

I stole. I did that?

Barreling out of the restroom, she started to rush to the donation box, but a group of adults in serious-grown-up suits blocked her access.

Screw. She pivoted and kept moving. Not running, not dragging her heels, either.

Martha was looking at her smartphone when Avery slipped into her seat at their workstation. For the first time since she'd seen Martha—both in person and pictured on internet gossip sites—the woman appeared sad.

"What happened?"

And *slam!* went the phone, facedown on the table. "Huh?" Martha said in a pretty awful impression of *puzzled*.

"The frown."

"Oh, I was thinking I'd hear from someone. A call, text." An I'm-saying-too-much head shake sent her curly hair bouncing around her face. "Forget it. We'll file it under Complicated Grown-up Stuff."

What could be complicated when you were twenty-something, wealthy, gorgeous and surrounded by hot athletes? *Oh...* "About a man," Avery whispered in a pretty awesome impression of *shrewd*.

Martha picked up a pencil. "And in *other* confusing topics, let's talk slope-intercept."

Guilt from stealing the donation-box shoes squashed her urge to laugh, but a smile managed to nudge its way to Avery's face anyway as she grabbed a sheet of graphing paper.

Around them, teens were matched with their tutors, escorted to meetings with counselors, encouraged to relax in the tripped-out rec room that looked like a converted solarium.

Faith House drew in system kids like her, who were in the way at home and whose families couldn't afford vacations and expensive activities. And it drew in those who de-fied the system—teenagers from the streets who ran away *to* Faith House because abusers, rapists, drug-pushers and pimps were on their heels.

Avery, who'd never been beaten, never given drugs, never molested, felt guilty for using resources that the street teens needed even as she feared she was on the brink of becoming one of them.

She might, if she jumped the foster-system nest and couldn't fly in the world on her own. She would, if she stayed much longer at Renata's or waited for DFS, her guardian, to take her away.

"Avery?"

Darting around, Avery realized she was clutching the graphing paper in her fist. She might've lost her lunch, had she spent her money on food instead of adding it to her Get Out of Las Vegas fund.

"What's wrong?" Martha asked.

"Nothing."

"Nothing?"

"Yeah, nothing. File it under Complicated Teen Stuff."

"Worried about what's going to happen next?" Martha set down the pencil. "Your foster mom's nurse said a so-cial worker's managing your case."

How'd she know that? Oh, no. "You called Renata's nurse?"

"I wanted to make sure you won't fall through a crack—"

"I *needed* that crack to fall through, Martha!" Avery's chest started to heave. "So I can get away."

"Wait, wait," her tutor pleaded, but the blood was whooshing through Avery's ears and she was shaking and people seated around nearby workstations began to stare. "There are so many foster families in the county that can give you a safe environment—"

"You're just parroting generic definitions of what fos-ter care should be. Well, it's not that way for every kid."

"This system matched you with Renata."

"There'll never be another foster parent like her. I'm thirteen, anyway, and I can run away." Pushing back in her chair, she started grabbing her books.

"Avery, we care—"

"Lie. You *don't* care, because you can't understand. And why should you care? You're living the dream life. Money. Parties. Friends. I don't have any of that. Or a subscription to *Vanity Fair* or 'complicated grown-up' problems. Or designer shoes." Avery dragged the clogs from her bag and threw them onto the table. "I stole these from the donation bin!"

Martha's jaw went slack for a moment. "Keep them."

"What?"

"I donated those shoes. Put them back in your bag."

Avery knew she shouldn't want to hold on to anything that belonged to Martha, but she found herself snatching them back.

"We've got to talk this out."

"No, Martha. Enjoy your dream life, and stay out of mine."

Avery bolted. It wasn't late, but the sky was dark and the chilly air piercing on her tear-streaked cheeks.

Forget Martha Blue and Faith House and everyone who pretended to care. No one would ever really listen. No one would ever understand.

No one would save her.

But she had her dream life in a binder, cash in her bag and a plan.

All she had to do was keep running.

Chapter 11

Fans weren't particularly supportive of the Slayers coaching staff and operations team's decision to rest three of their big-draw players—including the starting quarterback—in the final regular season game.

Martha, who'd followed along at home—studying play-offs scenarios and tracking the team's performance throughout the season during her downtime in S-Dubs—had come to the stadium expecting the head coach to go that route, and for the GM and owners to be in total agreement.

The majority of the league followed the school of thought that believed the practice of resting uninjured players attracted negative karma and took for granted the final regular season game. Able-bodied players should play; drawing backups increased risk of injury to men who'd be essential to play-offs emergencies. It wasn't in the men's best mental interests to approach a game knowing they weren't going to take to the field.

In true Las Vegas spirit, the Slayers opted to take the risk to give Dex Harper additional time to prepare for a play-offs offense under new leadership. Since he'd been reinstated as quarterback several weeks into the season, and had come home to an almost completely new coaching staff, he'd been adapting much of the season—and winning games while doing it.

Egos were bruised at the insinuation that the rested players were too valuable to use in a game that wouldn't change their position in the NFC divisional round, while the back-ups weren't as vital and could be gambled.

But that was business. Getting backup men onto the field in a regular season game offered visibility they wouldn't ordinarily enjoy—something that not only helped management gauge their effectiveness, but potentially would increase the players' value when it came time to trade and negotiate contracts.

Front office details never floated over her head—contrary to what many inside the organization believed. Sure, the misconception enabled her to observe certain operations functions, yet the preparation for the Blues' and the Las Vegas Slayers' response to the soon-to-break development in the Alessandro Franco investigation emphasized her need to be a part of the inner workings of the franchise.

With her sister Charlotte remaining rooted in her role as a trainer, and Danica no longer affiliated with the team—besides, of course, being the owners' daughter and the quarterback's lover—the owners were unhappily without an immediate relative to groom for the front office.

Meanwhile, Martha wanted to break free of S-Dubs, like one of the Slayers' primed players on the bench waiting to be called into the game.

Those primed players would get their chance today, but still she waited. She could appreciate that her "bench" was a cushiony chair in a tiny but stylishly decorated office.

And she was allowed access to the exquisitely appointed owners' box, which served as her perch now, as she nibbled caviar and gave the field a perfunctory scan. Several thousand ticket holders were in the bleachers—many of whom were already taking their bait-and-switch complaints to social media.

Mobility in her career was a concern close to her heart, but wasn't she one of the lucky ones? Every day she brushed against people who were more than sociological statistics, people who were evidence of a structural dysfunction in society. People who were forced to play the hand they were dealt.

People like Avery Paige, who'd the other afternoon literally run screaming from Martha's ineptness.

Was this heartache what her sister had intended when she'd offered a mansion in exchange for Martha's time?

Heartache blows.

It was a miracle that Faith House counselors and local police had recovered Avery late that night. She'd been collected from Hadland Park and returned home safe, sound and royally pissed off.

Another miracle? That Martha was still standing, because she was certain she'd stopped breathing the second the kid had burst through Faith House's doors and disappeared into the dark.

Afterward, Martha had wanted to go to Joaquin and be held. She'd wanted to lean on him even though he still hadn't called her or answered the text message she'd sent the day after Christmas.

So glad I found you under the mistletoe.

One-night-only sex didn't warrant day-after contact. People hooked up without exchanging phone numbers or even names. What an amateur move she'd made, but then, she *was* a little rusty in this department.

It had been months since she'd slept with anyone. And there *was* the nugget of a detail that she loved Joaquin Ryder.

Loved him and was in love with him—against her better judgment.

Martha didn't wait for the server to take up her silver saucer. She set it on an empty cart and walked over to the bar, where her mother and a few VIP guests were chatting over champagne.

Modeling Oscar de la Renta, with her jewelry glittering

and her smile so perfect, surrounded by refined pillars of high society, Tem was too stunning to disturb.

But Martha was almost weak with a despair she'd never tasted before and didn't totally believe was real. "Ma."

Tem swiveled on her leather stool. "You don't have a drink. That can't be right." She smiled beautifully, not realizing the light joke was so, so sharp. "Barkeep, you'll get my daughter what she wants?"

"He can't," Martha cut in, plopping onto the stool beside her mother.

Tem blinked, gracing the bartender with a confused glance. "Pour her a glass of what we're having."

Martha accepted a flute of champagne, took a gulp and set it down. She felt sorry that her efforts to help Avery had backfired, that their friendship was dead in the water and that the kid felt she had no one to protect her. Martha didn't want to imagine losing her mother. "Ma, your daughter wants to sit with you."

"The game's starting soon. Don't you—"

"Nope. Just sit here a minute," Martha said, scooting close and snuggling Tem's arm. "Y'all can keep talking."

Please don't give me the brush-off. Sometimes a girl needs her mother's attention, any way she can get it.

Martha felt Tem's sigh on her hair. Then Tem reached up to pat her cheek and grinned for her guests. "Occupational hazard of being a mother. Makeup smudges on your dress, courtesy of your adult daughter."

A few of the others laughed and someone pointed a phone to snap pictures, but Martha didn't care what Tem said, she wasn't letting go.

As more guests filled the suite, Martha stayed put, resting against her mother.

"There's something attached to your arm, Tem."

Martha recognized her father's voice dominating the noise of the crowded suite, but only nestled in more securely, quietly observing.

"It's a pretty accessory but clashes with my dress," Tem said.

"Is Coach Claussen catching hell out there?" Martha asked her father. If he wasn't already, she supposed the head coach would face a barrage of questions postgame.

"Yes, but he holds his own. Our fans want a stronger performance in the divisional game more than they want another regular season win."

"And here we are, prepared to deliver both," Tem added confidently. "Marshall, you did ask Claussen to stress the importance of rest to our QB?"

"There'll be a conversation, which Dex will pass along to Danica."

Stress the importance of rest...?

Martha jolted up. Realizing people were gathered within earshot, she kept her incredulous shriek to a whisper. "Ma. Pop. You *do* mean rest as in simply not playing tonight?"

"We mean we need Dex and Danica to make certain he doesn't overexert himself. On field and...off."

Martha coughed. "Cut down on sex? You're asking them to cut down on sex?" So *everyone* knew how often and energetically they went at each other. "Awkward."

"Protecting our QB's health's necessary," Marshall defended.

Martha took back all the times she'd yearned out of jealousy to trade places with Danica. Some sacrifices were necessary. "It's business, I suppose."

"I appreciate you viewing it that way." Her father gave a slight nod of...respect? Then he retrieved a bottle of sparkling water from behind the bar and used it to chase the pair of aspirin she hadn't noticed he'd carried.

"Headache?"

"Old-man ache."

Tem chuckled. "You and I are on the same level. If you're an old man, then that makes me—"

"Everything I want in this world."

Guests applauded and cheered for the charming response. It was smooth, and kind of poetic for big, tough Marshall.

He walked around the bar to grasp Tem's hand and they stepped away to take their seats at the windows.

Martha didn't intrude. So there it was. Her parents were profoundly in love. Her sister and the quarterback were having potentially dangerous amounts of sex.

And she was a woman irredeemably in love with a man who never was and never would be hers.

Yeah, heartache definitely blew.

Sliding off her stool, she worked the suite, flitting from one conversation to another, until she settled to watch the game.

At halftime, with the Slayers at a comfortable 24–7 lead, Marshall handed her an attractive black envelope with a silver wax seal. "Tem and I reserved a VIP table at that dessert bar in my club building. Grand opening's tonight."

The Grey Crusade was a private club to a limited number of the city's elite, and so exclusive that the ground-floor restaurant—and, apparently, the new dessert bar—were invitation-only.

Martha had ventured onto the premises only once, wiggling her way in without her parents' knowledge and indulging in an evening of billiards, wine tasting and nighttime golf.

After that debacle, they'd all but banned her from the place, so she was considerably intrigued to now have a sleek TGC envelope in her hands.

"Your father's feeling a bit under the weather, so he and I are handing off the invitation," Tem explained. "It's supposed to be a gorgeous, sultry place. Not as risqué as your usual go-to clubs. A nightcap there will be a tame change of pace for you."

Appetite, the new bar inside The Grey Crusade, was one of the absolute last places Joaquin wanted to be tonight. After Christmas, he'd intensified his workouts, bringing his stamina and endurance to unprecedented levels.

Uncle Jules had advised him today to bring things down a few notches and tap back into this newly achieved mode closer to the fight. So he was supposed to calm the hell down, stay mellow. But a dessert bar wasn't the place for him.

His cousin Tor and his wife had all but pleaded with him to hang on to the envelope he'd received, luring him to the grand opening event featuring exotic desserts and live jazz music.

It hadn't been an inconvenience to send someone to the restaurant on his behalf and secure two additional invitations for his cousin and his wife.

The inconvenience hadn't come until he'd actually walked into the bar.

Washed in grays, silvers and streaks of red light, the dessert bar offered brick bar-height tables and no seating. None. Customers interested in sitting were encouraged to do so in The Grey Crusade if they were members—or any number of bars Las Vegas had to offer.

At least the jazz band had chairs.

The table's lights centerpiece created exaggerated shadows on their faces, and with his thick goatee, Tor looked straight-up creepy. "Joaquin, Othello's with Ciera tonight. Thought you should know."

"Their choice." Easier to say than accept.

"No rage?"

"Fresh out."

Tor said to Brit, "This man effed up a heavy bag at the gym."

Brit looked to him. "What does that mean?"

"It means," Joaquin said casually, "I gave Uncle Jules enough cash to cover the cost of a new bag."

"Plus a new pair of sweats, 'cause I'm pretty sure he pissed his." Tor reached around his wife to slap Joaquin's shoulder. "Man, let me tell you what. Whoever was in that building left with *zero* doubt about who's going to leave the Garden Arena a champion."

"Let them doubt. It doesn't change what I need to do and how I get it done."

Brit slid her phone from her purse and started swiping and tapping. "Someone posted the vid online." Then she swore, the word hardly audible over the live band's saxophone. "Um, Joaquin. If you intend to do to Eliáš Brazda what you did to that bag, tell me so I can stay home with all the TVs off."

He laughed. "Brazda's more durable than that."

A waitress finally delivered menus and silk napkins, then another followed up with two bowls of strawberries.

A sexy long-legged woman whose every feature was now imbedded in his memory waved from a few tables away. "Not that I don't love jazz, but I'm calculating the probability of being fed before midnight."

"Come over," Brit encouraged. "We have food."

"Truly? I was beginning to think *food* was a glorious myth here." Martha discreetly met Joaquin's eyes through the shadows. *Is this okay with you?*

In answer, he shifted to the side, and then she was beside him in a silver dress that hung off one shoulder. Tor and Brit were on the opposite side of the tall brick table.

Brit slid a bowl of strawberries to them. "Tonight must be exciting for the Blues. Congrats on the win."

"Thank you," Martha said graciously. "I'm celebrating by starving in a restaurant called Appetite."

Tor and Brit chuckled, but tension coiled around Joaquin and he remained silent.

"Tough crowd." Martha glanced away from him and gave the couple a soft, hesitant smile. "My jokes are usually funnier. The extreme hunger is messing up my delivery. I could grab a fast-food burger and come back on *fiyah*."

"Don't mind the beast beside you," Brit said, teasing. "We're sticking out the grand opening experience."

"Brit's going to be the first one to give up. Heels this high." Tor held his hands a good six inches apart. "Or it might be Joaquin. All-day workout topped off with heavy-bag murder."

Before Joaquin realized what was unfolding, Martha had Brit's phone in her hand and was replaying the video. "What'd the bag steal from you?"

It was a joke, but he heard the seriousness hidden in her words. "It's just what fighters do, Martha."

His duty was to remember what he was, to make sure *she* remembered. The text message she'd sent him the day after Christmas remained dangerous and erotic on his phone.

It triggered memories of her pliant body in his bed and her naughty mouth on his skin.

You might be good to her, but you're not good for her.

But the thought began to fade when he shared his menu with her, continued fading as they ordered dessert and hard liquor, disintegrated completely when she splintered him with one of those rich arm-patting laughs.

Life was laughter and flaws and dreams for Martha. She weakened his resolve, but at the same time strengthened some other indiscernible part of him.

She loved. She trusted.

She was brave that way, and he a damn coward underneath his cold perfection.

His phone vibrated, and he darted a glance from the screen to the woman beside him. Her fingers sheltered her phone, and she was carrying on a conversation with Tor and Brit.

Forget what I texted about the mistletoe. I made you uncomfortable?

Joaquin inconspicuously replied, Turn my way and answer that.

Noticing her phone glow beneath her palm, he angled his hard body toward her and responded to something Brit said.

A soft vibration had him checking his phone.

We said one night.

Quickly, he typed.

Were we wrong again?

A subtle glance through the candlelight, then Martha was turning her phone facedown on the table and going for a bite of her gooey dessert.

Okay. Just because he'd asked didn't mean he would get the answer he wanted.

Swiping a chilled strawberry, he bit into it and watched her address Tor's question about wild-card weekend.

And he stopped chewing as his periphery found her fingers slipping carefully off the table and drifting to his crotch.

Oh, damn... Swallowing, he studied her profile as she explored the front of his pants with firm, quick strokes. Zipper to thigh. Harder, slower.

Taking another strawberry, he brought it to his mouth and used the other hand to cover Martha's.

One night. Christmas night. It was supposed to release him, yet it hadn't.

Joaquin stared at the curve of her lips, stole a glimpse of

that tight, rounded ass. One night of feeling the silky softness of her thighs, of taking hold of her mouth with his, of hearing his name on her shattered moans?

No, he couldn't go out like that.

Rays of candlelight streaked Martha's face, but he had a perfect view of her bottom lip rolling between her teeth then reemerging wet. His hand tightened on hers, then he moved it off his crotch.

A heartless bastard, a machine, shouldn't be this caught up. He shouldn't want her more than he'd wanted his ex-fiancée. He shouldn't be thinking she was right for him, because he wasn't right for her.

Facing the table again, Joaquin knocked back a shot and let his cousin lead him into a conversation about the pre-fight media workout.

"Repeat what you did at the gym today, and they're going to lose it," Tor predicted, taking down a third shot. "What brought that on?"

"Want."

Tor and his wife wore surprised expressions, while Martha seemed to be strangely close to tearing up the way she had at her parents' dinner when he'd given her a candy cane.

"Want?" Brit repeated. "Wanting to win?"

"Wanting something I can't have."

His cousin gave a snort of disbelief. "That Venom you took out on Christmas says you've got just about everything you want."

"Just about." Joaquin reached for a napkin, seizing an opportunity to touch Martha's hand—the hand she'd just had on his body. Her fingers grazed his.

"Quite a motivator," Brit commented, and breezed on to praise the coconut concoction on her plate.

That launched a conversation about food, and Joaquin hung back, preoccupied with the way Martha's palms lay flat on either side of her dessert plate.

Fixated on her, he reached for a strawberry. Pinched the luscious, supple fruit between his fingers. Cautiously brought it down, over the edge of the table…lower still, until he brushed Martha's thigh.

Watching her fingers splay, he knew her thighs were imitating the movement. He envied the strawberry as it skimmed her. When it reached her core, he maneuvered the string of lace aside and nudged the strawberry deeper.

Martha's fingers curled; the tendons on her hands tautened. He stroked her with the fruit, not stopping, not retreating, until her hands started to shake. And when she gripped the table, he felt her control slip.

"You okay?" Brit asked Martha, squinting through the jump of candlelight and glaring beams of red light crisscrossing the bar.

Martha's gaze landed on his.

As slickly as he'd maneuvered the strawberry off the table, he brought it up…and bit into it.

"Oh." Unsteadily, she rubbed her throat. "I—I need to get some, um, air."

Joaquin laughed.

"Want me to walk with you?" Brit offered.

"Finish your dessert." Martha plucked a strawberry from the bowl, started to stagger toward the exit. "Joaquin can take me."

"Want me to?"

A solemn, powerless nod. "Yes."

Taken. That was exactly it. She was taken. So was he. Completely captured, too far gone.

And so damn wrong.

They made it to The Grey Crusade, escaping to the arched recessed wall of a corridor boasting a wrought-iron art easel displaying a concert announcement.

It hit the floor with a clatter, bumped off balance from the impact of Martha's butt as she scaled Joaquin.

What passion was this? It infused her with a wildness and defenselessness she'd never encountered, couldn't handle. It bit, scratched, raged. All she could do was grip and ride—the passion *and* the man who tempted it. One arm around his shoulders, the other pulling his shirt, she said through ragged sighs, "I wanted to move on. I wanted to let go."

"Not yet," he growled, pushing her dress up to clutch her ass as she folded her legs around his waist. "Not while I'm still here." He kissed her hard. "Not when I can't let you go, either."

"Okay." She'd break her own heart to give up a few more weeks of this…of him. Flesh to flesh, vulnerabilities exposed, nothing to hide except her love. "After the fight, we stop being crazy."

His mouth on her neck, his hands tight on her bottom as he buried himself deep inside her, he echoed, "After the fight."

Chapter 12

Lockdown sucked. Avery's foster mom had never been as livid as she was the night Avery had run away from Faith House. Renata was so weak that some days she couldn't leave her bed, but on that night she'd had her son chauffeur her through Las Vegas, searching, until Avery had been found.

If Avery had planned every detail right, she would've had a solid head start—would've gotten much farther than Hadland Park, where she'd caught a side stitch and had cried herself to sleep.

DFS was on her ass, and now that school had resumed, counselors were stalking her—showing up in her classes, haunting the cafeteria, making sure she wouldn't bolt.

Renata had grounded her, restricting her to the condo and school. No television, which meant no Food Network. No Faith House, which was all gravy, anyway, because she'd be too mortified to show up there again. Who'd welcome her back after she'd stolen a pair of shoes from a donation bin and bitch-screamed at a tutor?

The only benefit to her epic fail was that Patrick had backed off with the rude comments and general asshattery. Maybe it had something to do with social workers crawling the place like ants. Or maybe he realized that she wasn't going to stick around to be picked on anymore.

So today, when Patrick had given her cash and asked her to bring home tacos after school, she'd been jazzed to kiss lockdown buh-bye.

Enjoying freedom, she ordered Patrick's takeout and an extra taco for herself, sat alone at a table in the restaurant and ate as the sunset died outside the window.

The taco restaurant's distance from the condo tacked an extra fifteen minutes to her commute, but Patrick could warm up his food or eat it cold. After she handed over the tacos and his change, she would check on Renata then finish her homework in her bedroom.

At the condo, she set the tacos and money on the entryway table, hoisted the strap of her textbook-stuffed tote bag over her shoulder and found the place oddly quiet. Between Renata, her son and her nurse, Avery was never left alone.

Where was Patrick? The nurse?

Walking through the living room, she did a double take. Her blood iced.

No... An interior door was propped against a wall, missing its hinges and knob. A few feet away lay the knob. It was brass, with a lock.

Avery's instinct was to go straight for the front door, but she instead thundered through the condo to Renata's room. She'd wake her and finally show her who Patrick was.

Barreling into her foster mom's bedroom, she skidded to a stop. Renata wasn't there. "Renata?" Crap, why was her voice so shallow? Why did her stomach hurt so much? *"Renata!"*

Swallowing past the fear in her throat, she went to her room. Relief soaked her. Her stuff—what was left of it, anyway—remained how she'd left it all this morning.

Jostled from behind, Avery tripped into the room. *"Hey!"* Regaining her balance, steadying herself on the desk chair, she glared at Patrick. "Where's Renata?"

"With her nurse. The tacos are cold."

"Use the microwave," she said, her voice so uneven she hardly recognized it. "Put my door up."

"Can't bring home a decent taco. Can't go to tutoring without causing a scene. Can't keep yourself out of trouble." He advanced, crossing the threshold, catching her by the front of her jacket. "Avery Paige. What *can* you do?"

"Leave." That's what he'd better do, and if he didn't, she would—and she would *never* come back. Whatever safety she'd once had here was gone.

"No, Avery."

Run.

Flinging the chair at him, she spun and raced for the fire escape.

Martha was bringing a crowd to Club Indiscretion, the nightclub and pavilion hosting the Las Vegas Slayers' pre-divisional game celebration. The last member of her party to be collected, she was met with a chorus of cheers when she sashayed out to the Hummer limo in a couture snake-skin minidress, her tallest stilettos and a row of diamond biceps bracelets on one arm.

The vehicle was roomy and plush and provided ultra comfort for her guests. Settling in between Soixante Neuf waitress Odette and Leigh Bridges's boyfriend, Bart, she asked the group, "How *do* I look?"

"Hot," Bart said, and when his girlfriend laughed, he added, "She asked." Confused, he rubbed the back of his neck and looked to Gideon, the only other male, with a shrug that pleaded, "Help me out here."

Gideon glanced at his date Chelle. "Is it kosher to tell a girl she's hot in front of your date?"

"Depends on your date." Chelle, who'd quickly given up her forced crush on Enzo the cook, had come to Martha's office to beg for an insta-date for the company celebration. Since Gideon was usually up for anything with free drinks and hot music, he'd been all good with coming to Las Vegas for the weekend and escorting Chelle and Odette.

In fact, as he eyed Chelle now, he appeared a little *too* all good. Martha found herself in a predicament, securing Chelle a date without being upfront about her friend's true sexual orientation and struggles with labels. Chelle's issues were hers to publicize or keep under lock and key, but there was Gideon to consider, too.

As the conversation coasted over Martha, she thought back to her own struggles with labels when she'd felt too alone and afraid to empower herself. *All water under the Brooklyn Bridge,* she liked to think when the memories seeped through. Must've staunched them too late, because she suddenly didn't have a taste for the limo's appetizers and booze.

Club Indiscretion was all class and promiscuity, stamped with the sponsor's silver-and-bloodred team colors. Gourmet food was available inside the nightclub, and both it and the pavilion offered an array of liquor.

Security combed the premises and bouncers flanked every entrance, but determined paparazzi still finagled their way inside to be hustled out again.

Tonight was not only a celebration of the team's accomplishment, but it was to Martha a reward to reap for the hours she'd invested in securing the concert headliner.

Yesterday at the administrative building, her parents had journeyed to S-Dubs to shake her hand in commendation for the accomplishment and her apparent attitude that only the best was acceptable for a Slayers event.

Martha *had* worked tirelessly to get what she wanted, but in the end, DZ Haze's stubbornness had forced her to call on the ace up her sleeve.

Hair tamed into a Grecian-inspired style and makeup unflawed, Martha walked through the nightclub to greet her ace with a warm smile. "Glad you could make it," she said to her ex-brother-in-law, Marion Reeves.

Personally, she thought him an unfaithful asshole deserving of someone who was exactly like him. Yet professional interests begged her to shower the music mogul with respect. He'd influenced DZ Haze to honor his commitment to the event, and Martha had invited him and a guest to a gratis VIP night.

Only, as she realized the congregation of suited men and refined women behind him *were* his idea of "a guest," he was intending on getting the absolute most of the courtesy.

"You didn't tell your people that *I'm* a part of the VIP experience, did you, Marion?" she asked him discreetly after a third man in his party tried to spirit her off to the dance floor.

"No," Marion denied. "They see a beautiful young woman and wanna know what's wrapped up in that tight dress."

"That's for me to know and no one here to find out," she said.

"I don't roll with scrubs," Marion told her. "Any of these men deserves a good woman. Marshall and Tem raised three, and you're the last one standing single."

"Didn't you let one of them go?" she returned pointedly, but in the sweetest of tones.

"That'd be the one coming up behind you now?" Marion bowed slightly and the club's lights glared down on his bald head.

Martha steeled herself for the fallout, but hoped Danica wouldn't ream her out in a jam-packed nightclub during a team event.

But Danica marched past her. "Marion, you and your group need to leave. The Blues are sponsoring an event here tonight. Club Indiscretion's closed to the public."

One of Marion's security hulks stepped forward. "Is there a situation?"

Danica's hip slipped and angry fire flickered in her eyes. "There will be if you don't leave this venue."

"Danni," Martha interfered, easing between the exes. "He's not part of the 'public.' He and his crew are, uh, they're invited guests. With a VIP booth."

"Why? Who did this?"

"I issued the invite. It was business."

Danica stared, dumbstruck, then shook her head and hurried off in the direction of the teeming pavilion.

Arranging for Marion and his guests to be well-handled during the celebration, Martha introduced him to a member of the event concierge team who'd personally attend to his needs. Glad she wouldn't have to deal with him further tonight—unless it was after too many vodka shots and she was yelling in great insulting detail her opinion on what he'd done to her sister—Martha wandered the spectacular grounds.

Briefly she found a safe haven beside the DJ, who was getting everyone hyped for the opening band. Then, when the opening performance started, she roamed until she claimed a seat at the pavilion bar. Seeing her sister pissed off had made her dizzy.

"Crowded enough for you?" asked Gideon, who remained standing when she gestured for him to park it next to her.

"Too. I got a little woozy."

"Or that boa constrictor's squeezing too tight."

Martha smoothed a hand down her dress, laughing gently. The wooziness lingered to a degree.

"Are you going to dance?"

"Probs. It's early yet. I was in too much of a rush to get a decent amount of food down," she said, though the delectable Bellagio spread at brunch with her parents and tonight's scrumptious celeb-chef catered offerings in the nightclub lacked appeal. Finicky from birth, she thought by now she'd gotten a handle on her idiosyncrasies and wouldn't let a tiny detail ruin her appetite.

"Dance with me later, Martha?"

Surprised, Martha sat straighter and retorted, "Chelle's not keeping you on your toes?"

"She and I stayed behind in the limo."

Oh, no. Chelle and Gideon went *that* far before they'd even stepped out of the Hummer?

Chelle was debating the version of herself she'd commit to. Gideon, with his suave charm and hankering for hotties, was on the fast track to playerhood.

"WTF face," he said. "Nice."

"Sorry."

"We *talked*, nothing more."

Martha twisted her mouth. "Is that the truth? Chelle's going to tell me eventually."

"She'll say it's not happening, the two of us." Finally, he sat beside her. "She's gay. She told me because, according to her, I'm the type to look at a woman and fall in love."

Now *that* was something Martha had never detected, and she prided herself on being very in tune with friends and family.

"Are you, Gideon?"

"Might be," he said thoughtfully. "She is."

Martha scrunched her brows. "What makes you say that?"

"The way she's been checking out your friend Odette since we got in the limo. The gang's doing shots in the club. Want me to have something ready for you?"

"Wow, look who's attentive." Martha laughed again, but he continued to watch her earnestly. "Guy, what's this?"

"Look, Martha. You think we could go back to Nantucket?"

Go back to Nantucket, as in re-create the wild, get-on-the-gossip-page weekend they'd spent last summer? So much had changed since then. *She'd* changed. They were strictly platonic friends now, and she was in love with someone else.

"Sweetie," she said, folding Gideon's hands in hers, "don't look at me and fall in love. Loving somebody who can't love you back? It's hell. Please, *please*, trust me on that."

Gideon's face contorted as he registered what she'd confided. "Um, does the guy know he's giving you hell?"

Shaking her head, Martha said, "Uh-uh, no."

"Don't you think he should?"

"It's just how things are, Gideon."

It was how things needed to be, if Joaquin was going back to his life in Miami, and she was going to one day find a man who'd give her a neat, uncomplicated storybook romance.

It wasn't ideal—it was what she'd tried like mad to avoid—but at least she had *some*one to love who loved her. Rabbit, her Christmas bunny, was a tiny miracle she hadn't known she needed.

"Go," she told her friend, slapping his hand goodnaturedly. "Party."

She left the bar, mingling with the press and team personnel as the opening band wrapped up their set onstage. Tem managed to flag her down on her way into the nightclub.

"Danica and I spoke," her mother said, steering her to a clearing.

Good news? They *were* speaking. Bad news? They'd likely bonded because both were upset with her decision to invite Marion Reeves to a team function.

"Ma, I didn't want to hurt Danica. But DZ Haze wouldn't be here tonight if not for Marion's influence. Inviting him to the event…I thought it was a necessary business move."

What lay behind Tem's regal, critical stare, Martha didn't know. "I respect that you found yourself faced with a difficult situation and took action."

"Was it the *right* action?"

"That's usually determined by the outcome, isn't it?" An enigmatic answer, but it lent much to consider. "You sound unsure of yourself. Confidence is vital in publicity, Martha."

Publicity. Of course. Because you still don't recognize

that I'm invested in this team beyond being the Blue daugh-
ter with a spot in S-Dubs.

"A publicist's image is vital, too. You've been flying
under the radar lately, which is appreciated. The franchise
doesn't need more inconveniences." A muscle tic between
Tem's eyebrows revealed controlled anger, which was expected, since Alessandro Franco's latest attack had become a part of the feds' and NFL's investigations and had
hit the media.

"Glad I could meet the publicity department's standards."

"It's progress."

Oh. So, no, she *hadn't* met standards. She'd made "progress."

"I should get back to schmoozing," she said, receding
into the swell of guests and event staff as heart-grinding
bass exploded and the massive LED screen lit with electric color.

Martha sampled appetizers, then let the intensity of DZ
Haze's extreme rap seduce her to dance—first with some
men from the team's defensive line, then with her sister
Charlotte, then alone in a simple sway.

A gravelly whisper on her neck stopped her completely.
"No stripper moves?"

"Aren't they meant for bedrooms and poles?" Instant
arousal had her skin heating with hyperawareness and her
thighs aching to be touched.

"Mmm," Joaquin groaned into her ear. "No. For me.
Your moves are meant for me."

Martha's head tipped back to rest against him and her
eyes closed. Spicy cologne teased her; the hardness of him
felt both safe and sinful.

You're too close. She should say the words, remember
where they were and what was at risk. But the desperate,
gotta-have-you passion rendered her silent.

She wanted him to strip off her snakeskin, own her with

his body, his hands and tongue and teeth. Compete for her, instead of conceding to her fairy-tale fantasies.

Scraping the diamonds circling her biceps, he said, "There's an after-party, right? I can be there—"

"My place," she interrupted. "You can help me take down the Christmas decorations. Then you can help me take down my hair. *Then*—"

"Martha."

She giggled at the pleading groan, turned around and almost jumped him. With her back against him before, she hadn't known he was wearing a silver-gray shirt, dark jeans and sunglasses.

If he grinned, if that dimple appeared, she was going to take off with him.

"Your purse is vibrating."

Martha lifted her handbag and dug out her phone. Unfamiliar number. Engulfed in rap music, she couldn't hear a word the caller said and shouted "Sorry!" into the phone before disconnecting the call.

"Couldn't hear. I'll let them call back and leave a message." But the phone buzzed softly once, then stopped.

"Oh, a text."

"Take care of that," he said, turning to leave her with her phone.

She opened the text. There. Again. Heart-stopping fear. "Joaquin, wait!"

He pivoted and was there when she almost collapsed. "Give me the phone."

Wordlessly, she showed him the text.

It's Avery. Help me. I'm sorry about the shoes.

"Avery? That kid you're tutoring?"

"Was. I *was* tutoring her. She's pissed at me. But she's in trouble." Martha squared her shoulders, bolstering herself, battling the returning wooziness. Should she allow him access to this aspect of her life? "You don't have to be involved—"

"Martha." Joaquin's arm banded around her, and she could lean on him if she needed to. "We're going to get her."

Lagoon Rock Road. The place was from Joaquin's past, and pushing the Escalade beyond its limits with his foot heavy on the accelerator and his hand tight on the steering wheel, he saw memories of neglected houses, barren yards, malnourished dogs, stripped automobiles and the flash of police cruiser strobe lights.

Mixed up with a group that had accepted him as a scrawny kid with the stones to do just about anything, he'd followed an order to hot-wire a car on Lagoon Rock and had ended up locked in juvie.

Over the next few years he was picked up in other neighborhoods for a variety of stupid shit from truancy to street gambling, but you never forget your first time.

Crime had been rampant back when he was beating those streets. The thought of a scared kid sticking to the shadows, trying to find her way to safety, triggered his instinct to protect. And somehow, the realization of how important she was to Martha made her important to him, too.

At the pavilion Martha had tried to give him an out that he hadn't taken. Wresting control of other folks' business was one of his unpopular fortes, and usually he didn't care. But Martha needed someone beside her, not leading her.

Tonight she needed safety and support. In the driver's seat, with one of his security specialists available at the touch of the Bluetooth speakerphone, he provided that.

When Martha had found out the kid was a ways from home and tiptoeing around on Lagoon Rock, she demanded his word that he wouldn't interfere with how she wanted to play this. No police or county family services ambushes. The girl—Avery Paige—didn't trust freely.

"Avery hopped a fence. She's in someone's backyard."

Clutching her phone, Martha twisted toward him in the passenger seat. "It's a wood fence with graffiti."

"Okay." Wouldn't narrow things down by much, but he could work with that. "Avery still on the line?"

She shook her head, swearing on a shaky sigh. "Phone battery's low."

"Text her. Ask her to stay where she is, if she can. Get low, watch and listen. Don't draw attention. She'll look like a target." Aware of the take-charge tenor in his voice, aware that she might figure he was being an alpha asshole about it, he kept talking. He knew Lagoon Rock and streets similar to it. The next minutes could take the kid's situation from critical to tragic if she got careless and detected on the wrong person's radar. "We'll get through to her when we get close."

Text sent, she waited motionless until a soft buzz sounded. "She texted 'okay,'" she said. "Spelled it out. O-K-A-Y. Most kids go for textspeak. Shortening words, sticking in numbers that sound like letters. Avery, she doesn't shortcut."

As she spoke, she started to relax, resting against the seat and loosening her grip on the phone. If he could keep her talking, it might hold the panic at bay. "What do you mean, she doesn't shortcut?"

"Avery commits. From-scratch recipes. Cleaning up the mess from one project before she digs into another. Solving algebraic equations using a paper and a pencil, instead of a calculator." Martha slanted toward him, calmer now. "She's had to adapt to so much. She's only thirteen. Somebody should've told her how smart and cool and tough she is. I should've."

"You can. Get her home—"

"Avery ran *from* home. Last month she hid in a park to avoid going home."

Joaquin frowned, easing the Escalade onto Civic Center Drive. "What's making her run?"

"It's not *what*. It's *who*."

"Yeah?" Still carrying some scars from the hard knocks he'd taken before he learned to defend himself, he had a special brand of loathing for people who terrorized kids. "Maybe somebody should introduce them to fear."

"Maybe someone will, but it won't be you. Avery needs care and consideration, not violence."

"She needs to be protected."

"Not through violence." Martha's hand curved firmly over his shoulder. "And you're good for more than that."

Was he? Fighting was the central purpose of his life. It was what he'd been trained and conditioned for. As his uncle had told him, he had no reason to stop fighting.

Joaquin didn't try to cut down her words or shrug off her grip. He loved her voice in his ears, how her touch radiated comfort completely through him.

He loved?

"Let's start looking for wood fences," he said, trying to catch the thought before it sank too deep. "And get her on the phone."

The ghost town atmosphere that welcomed them as they approached Lagoon Rock Road was familiar—as though he belonged to these streets. In a way he did. They were part of his past, something he'd survived.

Bringing down the speed, he navigated Lagoon Rock while Martha spoke in the phone. Suddenly she said to him, "I see her—about three houses ahead."

A slight figure was sliding down a fence, and met the ground with a wobble.

In a flash Martha disengaged the locks, he hit the brake and she shoved open her door. She jetted down the beaten sidewalk, leaving him to nose the SUV forward.

Joaquin got out, but stayed back, watching the grungy, waiflike kid outstretch her arms and stumble to Martha, bawling.

And something bright and weightless cut into him, the

way the headlights' beams carved into the dark street. A feeling that he was seeing a version of Martha Blue he'd never met.

That version of her stayed the night, shielding and encouraging Avery at the hospital, where she was treated for lacerations and a sprained wrist she'd earned tumbling off a fire escape. As no more than a friend of the kid's tutor, he was pushed to the fringes, overhearing bits of conversations as the hours drifted. A social worker, a pair of cops and Martha's sister Danica showed up.

"Avery's being released," Danica told him, meeting him at a cooler that offered lukewarm water.

"Back to her foster mom?"

"No. According to Avery's statement, her foster mom's son has been intimidating her for months and tried to assault her earlier yesterday."

"Piece of—"

"The cops are getting acquainted with him," she said, giving his biceps a firm clap. "Thanks for being here for Martha through all this. I'll get them home."

"What?"

"Your shift's over."

"What do you mean, '*them* home'?"

"There was a crapload of red tape, but they got their way. Avery's being released to Martha."

"Eliáš Brazda's going to beat you."

Joaquin, who'd been hitting the speed bag in a steady, accelerated rhythm, suddenly gripped it in his wrapped hands.

Adjusting his skullcap, he tracked Jules as he did a perimeter walk around the ring, then finally meandered to him.

"Brazda's not going to outclass you," Jules clarified, revealing a newspaper tucked under an arm. "He's going to beat you, hit you where it hurts. Because his camp knows you *can* be hurt. Here's your weakness, right here on the *Sun*'s front friggin' page."

Joaquin snatched the newspaper, making a concentrated effort to remain impassive, knowing his uncle was watching for a reaction. It wasn't easy, when his eyes narrowed on the headline Boxing Prince and NFL Princess Make a Royal Rescue.

Damn it. The press had been the least of his considerations when he'd escorted Martha and that scared, scraped-up kid to the hospital the other night. When he'd finally left, it had been only because he'd known they were safe with Danica.

Skimming the article, he saw more details about the Las Vegas Slayers' postseason celebration and his upcoming pay-per-view fight than his and Martha's "inspiring act of heroism." He figured it was because the hospital hadn't disclosed the kid's name, and the Blue family and his publicists had declined to comment. Good looking out.

"Uncle Jules, what's wrong with you? Relax, man." He passed back the paper and turned to the speed bag. "Shouldn't you be used to seeing my name in the papers?"

"Not hugged up with words like *heroic* and *compassionate*." Jules spat the last word, reaching up to block the speed bag with jittery hands. "Joaquin Sinner Ryder isn't a hero. He's a goddamn champion because he'll go through any man to win."

Adrenaline and anger moved through his system like liquid lead. He couldn't break momentum, couldn't slow down. Adapting, he swerved, targeting a heavy bag.

The unit he'd destroyed still hadn't been replaced. Which was odd, considering the pride Jules had always taken in this place and that he'd demanded cash to replace the damaged bag. "When're you going to get a new bag?" he grunted.

"One's on back order."

"Got companies in a pissing match to stock this place

with equipment," he said, mopping sweat off his forehead. "Why wait on a back order with that kind of money? Give me the name of the company. I can get a replacement installed—"

"Questioning me?" Jules growled, and Joaquin paused, noting the threads of red in the man's eyes.

He's tired, stressed, and it's breaking him. Desperate to believe that, he discounted the suspicions his uncle's anxiety and bloodshot eyes provoked. He rejected the memory of Martha telling him that Jules had been "jumpy" on Christmas. He tried his damnedest to not look at his uncle and see a trace of his mother.

"Want the money back?"

"No." The money Joaquin didn't miss. Jules was a grown man, his elder, his uncle, his trainer. But where *was* the money? In the gym's safe? A business account?

Jules raised you. He saved you. He gave you this life. Don't doubt him.

"I manage this gym *my* way, Joaquin."

"Okay, I can respect that. Now get out of my way."

Jabs, footwork, snapbacks. Stay graceful and merciless. Bar outside distractions—including his trainer—from his head.

But Jules was too close, interference he couldn't shut out. *Load that left leg going into the hit! Protect your chin! Bring down that elbow or you're open for the body shot that's gonna make Brazda champ!*

Jules came around, yanking the heavy bag to the side and hurling the newspaper to the concrete floor. "Anyone at Club Indiscretion that night could've gone with Martha."

"I was the one standing in front of her when the kid made contact. I was there, I had a car and I could protect them both."

"You're not that guy, Joaquin. The hero, the man to count on. You ain't built that way." Jules released the bag and it swayed slowly on the hook. "You're the reigning champ—the machine."

"The machine wouldn't save an innocent kid from getting done up on Lagoon Rock Road? The machine wouldn't protect his woman?"

"She can't be yours," Jules said wearily. "She's nobody's woman. If I believed what some folks say, I'd think she was everybody's woman."

Joaquin stepped around the bag, ready to defend, ready to damage. "When you talk about Martha like that, you're no longer my trainer, no longer my uncle."

Jules said darkly, "Your fight's not against me. It's not even against Brazda. It's against *you*." He bent to sweep up the front page of the newspaper. "You claim Martha now, but after MGM Grand, you can't give her anything. You're the champ because this life beats all else. My sons went for the marriage thing, but they're not champions. C'mon, man, you tried to have that life with India, and it almost screwed your name beyond repair.

"Martha's got her heels dug deep in Las Vegas with her family and the football team, and now she's got a runaway under her roof. You can't have the strings—not even a beautiful one like her."

Can't have. Restrictions, catches, limitations—he resisted them. A future that didn't intersect with Martha's looked hazy, vacant.

I don't want to lose her. Or the man I am when I'm with her.

"I'll defeat Brazda," he said, severing the confrontation. "But I'm not the machine."

"Then what the hell are you?"

"A man."

Chapter 13

In the days that followed since Martha had opened her home to Avery, the praise and criticism and questions ratcheted her annoyance to unimaginable heights.

The media wanted a piece of her any way they could get it—through family, friends, the Slayers, Faith House volunteers and even celebrities she'd been photographed with at various social functions.

They wanted the story, the salability of a Las Vegas party-girl washing her reputation clean by rescuing a system kid from skid row. Critics congratulated her "brilliance" while touting theories that it was no more than a damage control tactic to boost the Slayers' team image in light of new allegations of corporate corruption and misconduct.

Approaching the NFC championship matchup, the game that could usher the team to the Super Bowl, the Slayers needed hype and support.

Sports media outlets incessantly juxtaposed what was at stake for Las Vegas's pro football team and champion boxer. Potentially, both could claim victory within a week of each other.

The nation watched her, and wanted her to talk. Did she feel a sense of power to be at the core of Las Vegas's professional sports? Could she describe her relationship with Joaquin Ryder? Would she return the child she rescued to Clark County after the NFC championship game and after Joaquin's fight?

No, no and no. No, she didn't feel "power" in her designated role on the Slayers' publicity team, or as someone who'd never watched an entire Joaquin Ryder fight. No, she couldn't describe how or why she and Joaquin had let themselves become so complicatedly entwined with each other knowing it'd all unravel after his MGM Grand maincard event.

No, she would not return Avery to circumstances the girl feared, as though she was the publicity stunt cynics suggested.

Avery wasn't a story—she was a child so loving and loyal to her foster mother that she'd never asked for help.

Watching the girl sit in a treatment cubicle and list what her foster mother's son had done— frightening her, tampering with her bedroom door, throwing out her clothes— had sickened Martha to the point that she'd rushed to a restroom.

Then she had seen to it that Avery could make a choice. That Avery had chosen *her* was as surprising as the fact that despite how pissed she'd been at Faith House, the kid had trusted Martha enough to call her for help.

Giving Avery a safe harbor was the right action. No matter how dead-set her family was to prove she was wrong. Even Danica, who'd worked legal wizardry at the hospital, experienced a mini-freak-out when Martha announced plans to become Avery's caretaker.

Primed to tell off the next person who tried to control her life, she braced herself when Joaquin arrived at her gates. She'd been expecting her friend Leigh for dinner— and moral support for her first Big Parenting Moment.

Avery's health teacher had informed Martha that during the girl's absence from school the class had studied the human reproductive system. Martha imagined a classroom full of cringing and joking teens, but the teacher had implored her to do the responsible thing.

Since she'd never explained sex to anyone, she had made

good use of UNLV's library and LVCCLD and loaded her Audi with books on the subject. At the last minute, she'd decided it couldn't hurt to incorporate the sex-talk method her mother had used when Martha was a kid: using dolls as visual aids.

Agitated that Joaquin would choose now to swing by, when she had a BPM to tackle, she opened the door and said, "I decided I'm not a fan of the pop-in."

"The what?"

"Pop-in. Visits with no heads-up."

Joaquin gave her a steady look. "Martha, a foster kid's in your place. The county needs to check up on things. You're going to be getting good and familiar with the 'pop-in' as long as she's here."

Good point, damn you. "Well, that should ease up once I complete my training hours. I'm checking everything off my list. Fingerprinting, background check, home inspection—"

"You're committed," he said with enough sincerity to scrape away some of her preloaded grumpiness.

"I am. I was the minute I agreed to bring Avery here."

"I came here to ask if you're sure this is right for you."

"Please don't *you* try to talk me out of this. Everyone else I know has already tried and failed. I'm giving her the chance that Jules gave you when he took you in." She reached for his hand, and automatically their fingers laced. "C'mon in. I've been cleaning and sprucing things up. Avery tells me the house looks like a Pottery Barn catalogue. I'm thinking that's a serious compliment."

In the living room, Joaquin paused, dropping her hand. "A Christmas tree? You put up a Christmas tree after Christmas?"

"A *winter* tree." She explained what Avery had told her about Christmastime at her foster mother's place. Martha had bought the frosted artificial pine not to attempt to give the girl the holiday, but to offer the spirit of the season.

It had remained bare until yesterday when Avery had written the word *kindness* on a piece of paper, threaded a ribbon through it and hung it on a branch. Without comment, Martha had followed Avery's example, adding *forgiveness* to the tree.

Neither had added one today.

"Did someone make hot wings?" Joaquin asked, sniffing the air. "Wait...you cooked?"

"I did. Why do you sound turned off?"

"I've heard awful stuff about your cooking—" his laughter was low, teasing "—from you."

"Recipes, patience and the chef-in-training who lives here now are making a difference." Martha sighed when his large, strong hand found hers again. "Sharing my life with this child and Rabbit, it feels right. But I miss us."

It'd been too long since he'd kissed her, since he'd inspired her to consider something outside the fairy tale her life had suddenly deviated from anyway.

Husband, baby, puppy. She had a bunny, a teenage foster daughter and a lover who'd be swaggering out of her life in a couple of weeks.

Edging close, he repeated her words. "I miss us. There wasn't supposed to be an 'us.' But we couldn't beat this."

Send him off when no one could put that kind of need in his voice but her? Let him leave Las Vegas without telling him she loved him? How the hell would she do it?

"We were about to have dinner in the backyard, once my friend Leigh gets here," she said. "Say hi to Avery? She's been wanting to thank you for helping me rescue her. If she's superskittish, don't take offense. What she's been through..."

When she led him into the kitchen and Avery, who was still managing a sprained wrist, rushed him, Martha's choices were to leap off to the side or be smashed in the middle of a hug.

She leaped.

"Thank you," Avery said, squeezing Joaquin tight. "You care about people. On TV, they never say that."

Joaquin met Martha's gaze, laid a fist on his chest. A goner, just as she'd been when she'd traipsed into Faith House with takeout pizza from Soixante Neuf.

"I think he's hoping for a free meal," Martha told Avery. "Should he stay?"

Nodding, Avery pointed to the cooktop. "I'm making the sauce, from a recipe my foster mom—uh, Renata—taught me." She showed him a page in her worn photo album.

"Solid recipe," he commented. "Worcestershire—I respect that. Ever consider adding molasses? If you're not too worried about spiciness, you could make a decent zesty honey-molasses sauce."

Avery stared. "You can cook? Cook *well*?"

"I hold my own." With a grin for Martha that made her heart flip and flop, he asked Avery if he could check out the rest of her recipe collection.

And for the first time since Martha had met her, Avery beamed.

When Leigh arrived on her Harley, clad in black leather, Martha met her in the foyer with, "Dolls?"

Leigh feigned a smug smirk. "Def." She held up a Barbie and Ken, new in pink boxes.

"Great, now put them away. BPM has been postponed till after dinner. We have another guest."

"BP what?"

"BPM. Big Parenting Moment."

"Who belongs to the Escalade?"

"Joaquin Ryder."

"Why is America's sexiest boxer in your house?"

"He's a family friend and he wanted to see how Avery's holding up." That was *part* of the truth, anyway.

Excited, Leigh let out a tiny fangirl squeal, stuck the dolls behind throw pillows and proceeded to nab Joaquin's autograph for her boyfriend.

Over dinner in the custom-built-for-kickass-entertaining backyard, all had been calm and the conversation light until somehow they swung onto the topic of boxing legends.

Perhaps it wasn't *entirely* coincidental that Martha lost her appetite as she thought about the physical risks Joaquin would court in the ring with Czech Republic champion Eliáš Brazda and reminded herself that fight night would end her relationship with Joaquin. When nausea threatened, she excused herself to a bathroom until she could pep-talk herself to a more upbeat mood.

When she reemerged, she found Leigh and Avery facing Joaquin on the terrace, mimicking a boxing stance.

"Are you teaching them how to fight?"

Joaquin broke his stance to adjust Leigh's fist. "A few basic moves, a couple of pointers in awareness and confidence. It'll help them defend themselves."

"What about running?" She'd always run, could always count on her legs to take her away. They had before. "Escalating a situation with violence isn't the way."

"What if you *can't* run, Martha?"

Leigh tapped Avery's shoulder. "Dessert's in the kitchen, right?"

"Yeah."

"Then we should be in there." Giving Martha a raised-brow look that begged, "What's *wrong* with you?" Leigh ushered the girl inside.

"Avery escaped." She leaned against a stone column, resting under the wash of golden light from a sconce. "She ran. *I* ran."

"When?" Joaquin was in front of her, his expression grave yet pleading. "What happened?"

"New York." The words fell on a sigh. "Freshman year of college. I was at a bar with some friends. We flirted for drinks, but we weren't there to hook up. It wasn't the mission." She reached out to trace a button on his shirt. Concentrating on that button, she let herself speak again. "A man kept sending me drinks, but I got bored, and since my friends weren't ready to take off, I split. He followed me outside, tried to charm and guilt and threaten me into having sex with him."

Martha gripped the button. "All I could think was, 'No, he's not my choice. This isn't my choice.' When he hit me across the face, the violence terrified me. I ran. I got away."

"Name? Did you get the name?"

"So you can hunt him down?" She shook her head.

"I didn't get his name. The women I was with convinced me to shut up about it. They didn't want the university or our families to know we'd snuck into a bar. People would say the slut got what she asked for."

"You didn't ask to be followed and hit."

"It was a while before that really sank in. I promised myself that no one would take away my choices. When I came home for Christmas, I chose you. I *wanted* you."

Only her attempt at seducing him had splintered like crystal.

"Tabloids label me out-of-control, but I'm out of everyone else's control—not mine. Because I make my own choices. Sometimes they're not the best, sometimes they are." She shrugged, felt herself smile thoughtfully. "But they're *my* choices."

"Did you ever tell Marshall or Tem—"

"No."

"Martha—"

"It's a choice, to not know what they'd say. To not know if they'd blame me." She rocked forward, gearing up to walk away, but his arms opened and she found herself walking into his embrace instead.

"I don't blame you," he said.

"I know." *I'm not simple to understand and you're not afraid to try. It's a reason I love you.*

"Gotta get back to the gym, but think about this. Fight

or flight is a choice. Fighting's violent, but it's another way to protect yourself. If your friend and Avery want to see it that way, it's *their* choice."

As much as she craved to resist it, it was another good point. He seemed to have an endless supply of those.

After he left, Martha turned away from the door to see Avery behind her holding up the doll boxes.

"If these are for me, you should know that no one in my grade plays with these unless they'd like to be laughed at."

"Martha, problem. I can't find Barbie and Ken," Leigh called out before she stopped in the foyer. "Oh. Cancel that SOS."

"Please tell me *y'all* don't play with dolls."

Hell's bells. Martha took the female and handed Leigh the male, and they opened the boxes. "Okay, here's the thing, Avery. Your health teacher let me know you missed the sex ed lesson. I thought I'd, um, give you notes. The dolls are props."

"Props?"

"It's how I learned."

Avery scratched her head. She was sporting a wrap while her sprain healed, but Band-Aids no longer covered her cuticles. "I already know about sex. And—" she took the doll from Leigh and yanked down his swim trunks "—Ken has no penis."

Leigh dashed off toward the living room in a haze of black leather, but her cackling belly laugh could probably be heard next door.

"Can I go now? There's a new competition show on the Food Network. And can I bring Rabbit's cage into my room?"

Martha waved the Barbie in surrender. In the living room, she sat beside her friend. "Big Parenting Moment was *not* a success."

"Oh, I'm thinking you'll get another chance soon." Leigh picked up her purse, cocked her head to listen for the pitter-patter of a teenager's feet. "During the emergency doll mission, I, um, got something for you."

Then she yanked out a box and plopped it on Martha's lap.

A pregnancy test.

"Don't take this the wrong way," Leigh said hastily, pushing her dark hair behind her ears. "Cranky. Nauseous. Light-headed. You've been all of those things the past couple of weeks. Did you miss the end of your sentence?"

"No—wait—" *Oh, God.* "I'm late, but I figured it had to do with external stuff. My MBA program, Rabbit, Avery, the team."

"Take the test."

Holing up in her private bathroom while Leigh raided the closet—what was the point of friends having the same shoe size if they didn't share sexy footwear?—Martha followed the test instructions and held off panicking...

Until a positive result popped up on the test stick.

"Leigh!" Her friend rushed into the bathroom, glanced at the stick. "I can't breathe."

"Yes, you can, Martha."

"I cannot be pregnant. I—I have a foster kid and a rabbit and a house. I'm already doing the grown-up thing."

"Calm yourself."

"But how can I be *pregnant*?"

"I'm guessing your mom's idea of sex ed with dolls wasn't very effective."

Her parents had asked her to keep *away* from scandals. Only, she hadn't. She'd slept with Joaquin Ryder and was now pregnant. And when the public found out...

When her family found out...

When *Joaquin* found out...

"This stays here," she said. "How I handle this is my choice."

"But the father—"

"Won't be a part of this. He can't be. He's..."

"The man who left this house about an hour ago, isn't he?"

Martha closed her eyes, nodding. She wanted to deny it, but it felt unforgivably wrong to start her baby's life on a paternity lie.

Her baby.

Just a few weeks of secrecy until Joaquin left Las Vegas. It was all the time she needed to adapt to yet another change and cope with the reality that the fairy tale wasn't meant for her. Her reality was unconventional and full of surprises.

Before going to bed, she went to the winter tree, found a branch with the word *laughter* in Avery's handwriting, and smiled. She grabbed paper, pen and ribbon and waited for a moment with a hand pressed to her belly.

Then she wrote.

Surprises.

Foregoing her lunch break for a sandwich in the head coach's office and a visit to the owners' suite, Martha took a seat across from her father's desk. "Pop, I just reviewed some films with Coach Claussen, and I have a suggestion for the NFC championship game—"

Marshall raised a hand, fidgeting with his necktie. "Tem's not here to humor you and I don't have the energy today, Martha. We'd appreciate it if you'd apply your attention completely to the publicity and marketing floor. Claussen's office, the managers' wing and the owners' suite aren't where you belong."

"Didn't my suggestion to hold a meeting with the roster about the Franco claims prove valuable? Haven't our men's numbers been excellent compared to previous weeks?"

"Tem and I consulted our GM and coach and made a group decision to do that."

"Sir, it appears you're making deliberate efforts to ignore my potential and commitment to the team." Martha crossed her legs, folded her hands. "Is it not obvious by now that my interests are in business operations?"

Marshall sat forward, resting his thick arms on the desk. "An NFL team's business operations are a little off the beaten path for a new graduate who majored in communications."

"But not if that graduate immediately pursued an MBA program."

"What?"

"I'm enrolled at Lee Business School. Have been since the fall."

"But you're taking care of Avery—"

"And a bunny and a house and volunteer work." And a baby, in her womb, already relying on her. "I'm handling it, Pop."

"Where does your drinking and dancing fit in?"

Well, that stung, but she'd in the recent past given him cause to be concerned. "Part of adjusting is knowing when and how to shift priorities. My suggestions—the ones you've reluctantly listened to, the ones you've ignored—for this team have all been effectual."

"A few months of business school isn't enough to grant you decision-making power in this aspect of our franchise, Martha. It just isn't."

"What about twenty-three years of being your daughter? I grew up watching you and Ma surpass success. You bought this team to reach new levels of wealth and power. You want employees who take risks, who are…" Confident.

You sound unsure of yourself. Confidence is vital in publicity, Martha.

Vital in publicity, vital in business altogether. Had her mother been offering a clue in that smooth, impassive way that was uniquely Tem?

"Damn it, Pop, I'm not afraid to put in hard work, make tough decisions." She abandoned her chair and he stood, as well. Sure, give her courtesy when she was on her way out the door. "You *will* need me."

Martha grabbed the door lever as a sickening thud

sounded. Whirling, she saw sunlight streaming over marble and leather and glass. Marshall no longer stood with his hand extended toward the door.

He was crumpled on the floor.

Screeching for security, Martha sprinted to the desk, yanked the phone off its base and dropped down beside him. He couldn't be—not Marshall Blue. Not her father.

It didn't take long for the swarm to find them. Team physicians, accompanied by Charlotte in her trainer uniform, had reached the owners' suite shortly after security. A thready pulse was what Martha had felt, pressing two fingers to her father's neck.

Barely a sign of hope, but enough to cling to for Marshall's sake—for the sake of those depending on her to be resilient.

With Charlotte joining paramedics in the ambulance, Martha had let her friend Chelle drive her to the medical center, where Marshall was admitted. Instead of his high-profile status deterring media and prodding people to respect the Blue family's privacy, it had drawn a crowd.

The crowd was outside, in the lobby, trying to breach security blockades stationed at the elevators.

"You'd feel better if you sat down, at least for a second," Chelle said from the emergency room waiting lounge.

Martha lingered in the entryway, glimpsing faces and not seeing any of the people who'd wheeled her father away on a gurney. "Knowing Pop is going to survive this is the *only* thing that'll make me feel better."

"Tem is on her way, isn't she?"

Martha nodded. Tem had taken the jet to California for a magazine photo shoot and interview, but had cut everything short to get back to Nevada.

"And your sister Danica?"

"She's picking Avery up from school and bringing her here."

The sports program on the giant flat-screen television was once again interrupted with the breaking news that had been reported twice in the past half hour: Las Vegas Slayers owner Marshall Blue collapses at stadium. Condition not yet released.

Reporters rattled off "possible" details, commentators promised viewers up-to-the-moment news. They posed a question for social media debate: How do you think Marshall Blue's health will affect the Slayers' performance in the NFC championship game this weekend?

Martha had her own questions.

Where was humanity, the compassion for a man whose life dangled in the balance?

How could the media think they were entitled to information Martha didn't have?

How could she be relegated to an ER waiting area when she wanted to be as near to Marshall's treatment room as her sister Charlotte was?

"The team must release a press statement," Chelle said hesitantly. "I can handle this at the stadium if you don't—"

"I need to be involved. I want nothing official going out that my parents wouldn't green-light."

"Okay." Chelle stood, joined her in the entryway. "The best cardiologist in the area quit a golf game to come here and treat your father. That's a big deal."

Martha sighed, and tension eased. "Thanks, Chelle."

A soft buzz sounded and Chelle plucked her cell phone from her pocket. Quickly, she swiped the screen, tapped a response and pocketed the device. "Odette says she's sending you and your family good thoughts."

"I appreciate that…" Martha turned to her friend as realization slowly settled. "Are you and Odette friends now, or…"

"Or." Chelle's mouth trembled as it formed a hesitant smile. "The night of the party, at Club Indiscretion, I quit lying. I've been so scared, but at the end of all that fear was Odette. This thing between us, it's still new, though."

"But are you happy?"

Chelle's nod was slight, but certainty shimmered in her eyes. "Yeah."

"Maybe you should go and be with the person who makes you happy. Seems we should take every happy minute we can get, because…" Tears threatened and she stopped talking.

"Sit down, Martha. It might take off some of the stress. I don't want to see you getting all damsel-in-distress fainty the way you've been the past couple of weeks."

Would Marshall never meet his first grandchild? Why had she kept her pregnancy a secret? Why had she wasted time being afraid of a miracle?

"I'm pregnant."

"Who's— *Oh.* The guy you talked about at Soixante Neuf? The one you said is zero good for you?"

A nod.

"Does he know?"

A head shake. "He can't give me what I need, and here I am giving him what he said he doesn't want."

"How can you hold him to that, now that there's actually a baby—*his* baby—inside you?"

Martha had to. The other option? Muddy things further with talk of love and a baby and the fact that she wanted Joaquin the man, not Joaquin the boxer.

She couldn't force him to relinquish his entire life to be who she needed him to be. Sometimes love meant letting go.

"He should have a say, Martha."

"It's not that simple! I had a plan—a down-the-road plan. An uncomplicated husband, a baby and a dog, in that order. A month ago I was single and lonely. Now I have a bunny rabbit, a foster kid and a baby on the way." Tears licked down her cheeks, and she brushed them off. "I'm not lonely anymore, but I'm permanently and utterly in love with a man who, even if he *does* love me, doesn't want to. My father had a heart attack today. I'm simultaneously the happiest and most miserable I've been in my life."

"If you love this man, shouldn't he be here with you now?"

"I haven't told him, because love can be trouble. For anyone. Young, old, straight, gay, rich, poor."

Chelle hugged her. "Let's get you to your dad. Right now."

Navigating the emergency floor, they saw Charlotte slip into a treatment room as a nurse exited. Pulling the nurse aside, Martha gleaned her father had experienced a coronary artery spasm—and was expected to recover without complications.

Waiting outside the door, Martha knew she oughtn't listen to her sister's one-sided conversation with Marshall, but couldn't resist her eavesdropper's instincts.

"Pop, it's serious," Charlotte was saying, kneeling beside the bed. "I'm going to marry him…"

Was that Charlotte's secret?

Were all three Blue girls hiding something they should be celebrating?

Over the next hour, Marshall was transferred to a private suite, which then quickly became congested with family and business associates.

Together, Martha and Chelle worked from their smartphones to draft an official team statement to send to the head of their department for approval and release. While her father's suite was still bombarded with visitors, Martha found a quieter place to help Avery with her algebra homework.

Eventually, Tem arrived and stationed herself at her husband's bedside. Chelle offered to buy Avery dinner in the cafeteria, and Martha let them go, wandering into her father's hospital room and fully expecting to be ordered right back out.

Tem was disheveled, wrecked and completely beautiful. Sparing her daughter a brief glance, she returned her attention to a sleeping and heavily medicated Marshall. "You're the other half of me. You're my partner in everything. Who am I without you?"

"Without Pop and without any of your children, you're still you," Martha said, bending to wrap her arms around her mother. "Strong, complex Temperance."

Tem untangled herself from Martha's embrace. "When an already sensitive person becomes overemotional, this is the end result?"

"So what if it is? Ma, you have an identity that's independent of your marriage and motherhood."

"Oh, Martha. From the lips of a young woman who doesn't have the commitments of marriage and motherhood."

"But I will—at least one of them."

Tem's spine pulled straight, and she settled a pair of narrowed eyes on Martha.

"There's something you should know." Coward's way out, maybe, but Martha held her mother tight. Tem's strength made her buoyant, and if she lent her support instead of banishing Martha out of the family, then they stood a chance of getting through this.

"I don't think you should say more right now."

But she had to. "Ma, I'm enrolled at UNLV's business school."

Tem sighed, and her entire body relaxed as though someone had deflated her. "Oh! Oh, God, for a moment I—" she laughed, sniffled "—I worried, well, I thought you were going to say you're pregnant."

"And I'm pregnant."

Tighter, she clutched, but there was only resistance.

"Today you baited your father into a debate about your suitability for the front office, all while hiding a pregnancy?"

"Pop didn't collapse from having a conversation with his daughter."

"I'm sure your persistent nagging didn't assuage his stress. Do you not agree?"

Martha bit the inside of her cheek to keep her expression steady, to keep herself from crumpling. Marshall *had* urged her to drop the issue, but like both of her parents, she wouldn't back down. "If I'd known his heart was— Ma, I wouldn't purposely endanger Pop."

"So you say. You also say you care about what's best for business, but you do something so damaging to our company?"

Martha let her go, keeping her voice lowered and patient out of consideration for her father and because she didn't have the energy for anger when she wanted to rejoice. "I don't see it that way, and I didn't tell you because of this reaction precisely."

"An unplanned pregnancy, single motherhood? Do you know who the father is?"

"Yes, I do, because the spreadsheet you recommended has kept me very organized," she said sarcastically. "Ma, there's been only one man since this summer. One."

"Then you're in an actual relationship and it's not emotionless sex?"

What could she call what Joaquin and she shared? There was sex—plenty of it, and it was so mind-melting and boundary-crossing that they kept coming back for more. There were emotions—too many that ran too deep. "I'm in love with this baby's father, but he doesn't know there *is* a baby."

"Does he love you?"

"I can't say."

"You *can't say*? Who the hell is this man?" Tem's face scrunched in a genuine scowl, which Martha would venture to guess hadn't happened since before her pageant days. "Marshall and I were worried you couldn't last through play-offs without bringing on trouble. We were certain you'd ignore our warnings and satisfy whatever whim hit you."

"Yes, and you were planning to fire me from the Slayers after play-offs."

"Okay, so Joaquin talked. That's fine. A man has his reasons for the choices he makes. What would've been helpful, though, was if he'd actually protected you from this scandal. He gave his word that he'd keep you close." Tem stared up at Martha. "You and Joaquin *were* close, these past several weeks. But you managed a tryst."

"I let myself love somebody, Ma. That's all."

Tem's nostrils flared, and her attention momentarily shifted to something beyond Martha's shoulder. "Name, Martha."

"Trust me to tell him about the baby in my own way, in my own time."

"Hiding this man's child is the same as lying. But I can't persuade you otherwise. You wouldn't be in this hell if you valued my opinion. Just give me his name."

"Joaquin Ryder."

Disappointment and a snap of resentment flooded Tem's expression, then made way for cold satisfaction as she reached to turn Martha toward the man filling the doorway. "Well, Joaquin Ryder, I imagine you and Martha have something to discuss."

Joaquin's soul all but fragmented when he heard Martha name him—*him!*—as the father of her baby. Martha was pregnant.

He'd been in this place before, with his ex-fiancée, India. India had rushed to him with the news, and had started planning a baby shower right away. Martha had hidden her pregnancy until she found herself manipulated into revealing the secret with her back turned to him.

India had lied. Trusting her had been a pitfall.

He walked ahead of Martha to the patient suite's waiting area. "Charlotte, Danica, I need this room. Please."

Danica glanced up from a tablet. "What the hell for?"

"Martha's pregnant," he said, turning to look her square in the face as he stripped her secret bare. "It's mine."

"What?" Charlotte and Danica shrieked in unison.

Martha stared at him through those misty eyes that had nearly unraveled him before. This time, the tears spilled over, and he felt like the exact same bastard he'd been four years ago when he'd ordered her out of his uncle's gym.

"I asked if you and Joaquin were hooking up," Charlotte persisted. "You said no."

"We weren't then." Martha pointed at the door. "Besides, don't ask me to spill my secrets when you're not willing to spill yours."

"We were careful," he said when her sisters left the room.

"We weren't. Not at The Grey Crusade."

Damn it. He hadn't protected her. They had wanted each other, taken what they'd wanted and hadn't apologized.

"When were you going to tell me?"

"After the fight."

"After I'd left Las Vegas?"

"Yeah."

"How long after, Martha?"

Her jaw tightened. "I wasn't going to trap you the way India and Ciera tried to."

"No, you were going to keep my kid away from me. You say you trust me and feel so safe with me? Then why hide your pregnancy?"

"I can't be okay with the violence. I'm not scared of you. I'm scared *for* you. No one is invincible."

"I'm going to beat Brazda."

"After Brazda, there'll be another opponent, then another. And you'll keep setting these matches until someone stops you the only way you can be stopped. He'll destroy you. And I'm terrified that fighting means more to you than anything else. A baby deserves better than that. You should want me to have more than that."

"I do! I love you, damn it, Martha. I keep telling myself that you deserve a better man…more than I can give you. The freakin' fairy tale you talked about."

"The fairy tale is exactly that. It's not real. If you want me, you should be fighting to show me that life with you surpasses a stupid fantasy. It's not going to be a pleasant husband, then baby, then dog. It's all out of order—and I'm glad." Martha stopped batting at her tears. "This baby doesn't have to be a problem for you. He or she can be mine alone—"

"Hell, no. It's mine—"

"Hey," she snapped. "You won't stand here and start paring down my choices."

"And you won't steal mine." Joaquin stopped, rolled his shoulders. "Why can't *we* be an option? You. Me. Together."

"You can't walk away from the fight."

"Is that what you want? Me to throw the fight? Throw my integrity? Give Brazda my championship?" He was silent, but silence didn't pierce the tension. "Damn, what does it mean that I'd actually consider it…for you?"

"Don't consider it."

Joaquin drew her close, held her shoulders, felt her grip his elbows. And their mouths met, bypassing any gentleness or hesitation. Both knew what they sought; both feared they wouldn't find it even in a kiss.

"God, Martha. I love you."

"Love shouldn't tear us up. We should *want* this." She sighed. "Step back from this right now, okay?"

His hands slipped from her shoulders. Now he knew what defeat was.

At the door, he turned to her when she whispered his name.

"You didn't ask if it's your baby."

"No. I trust you, Martha. That's what this love is."

Chapter 14

Martha didn't think she'd be the first visitor her father would ask for once discharged to recuperate in the comfort of his home and under the care of a cardiac nurse and dietician.

Guilt said her presence would trigger another collapse—one that nitroglycerin and calcium channel blockers couldn't defeat—so she'd refused to hightail to her parents' home at the first summons.

The second summons had arrived via a crisp, emotionless text message from Tem, advising her to fold up her office for the remainder of the afternoon and pay Marshall the respect she owed him.

When she arrived at the mansion weighed down with fragrant flowers, she found a familiar Cadillac Escalade parked at the estate and sighed. Of course she wasn't the first visitor Marshall wanted. Of course her parents had only been lying low during his hospital stay, until they could unleash their wrath in more comfortable surroundings.

A housekeeper promptly relieved Martha of the flowers while another escorted her to the sunny breakfast room, where Tem sat regal in a wingback chair, sipping tea from a china cup. Clothed in a plain gray dress, with her hair gathered in a severe twist at the nape, she appeared subdued.

Pointing her cup at a pitcher of chilled milk, Tem said, "Care for a drink?"

"Guess so." When Tem sent the housekeeper to fetch a glass, Martha asked, "Where's Joaquin? I saw his truck."

"Discussing BioCures with Marshall and one of the lawyers. Business doesn't pause for life's uh-ohs."

"My baby's not an 'uh-oh,' if that's what you're indirectly saying."

Tem shrugged. "Whatever you say."

"No, not really, when it comes to you, Ma. How could you trick me the way you did at the hospital?"

Her mother rose, meandered to the doorway and waited for the housekeeper to return with the glass. Filling it halfway with milk, she gave it to Martha. "Are you keeping up with gynecologist appointments? Taking vitamins?"

"I am. And I asked you a question. Why, Ma?"

"I didn't tell Joaquin you're pregnant with his baby. You did."

"You set me up."

"It was a split-second decision, and it was for Joaquin's sake. I couldn't let you deprive him of being involved in his baby's life." Tem shook her head, somber. "I did the man a favor and he has the nerve to insult me."

"Insult?"

"Do the words *manipulative* and *disloyal* sound complimentary to you?"

Accurate, yes. Complimentary, no. "Seems he'd appreciate you having his back, and not mine."

"Well, that's exactly what he didn't appreciate. He's of the mind that I manipulated and was disloyal to you." Her brows quirked over her large, all-cried-out-puffy eyes. "At the hospital you couldn't say whether or not he loves you, but he took care of that today. Could be something he blurted out in the heat of the moment, with no truth behind it."

Could be. But Martha's intuition insisted it was the truth. He loved her, even if he hadn't intended to shout it at the hospital or blurt it to Tem.

"The NFC championship game is tomorrow. Marshall won't be there—doctor's orders. I need my unit to be solid. If the baby-daddy scandal could be contained until after play-offs…" Tem suddenly grabbed a linen napkin, jammed it against her eyes. Swearing, she whispered, "It's not enough that Alessandro Franco's targeting your father and me. Or that BioCures group is trying to put your father in a choke hold. Our daughters, one by one, are working against us."

"That isn't true. We're creating our own lives."

"I don't want this. I—I want *my* life. Before, it's like I had it all right here in my palm—" Tem made a fist, stared at it "—and I could hold my career and my family and my youth right here. But it's all being pried out of my hand now. My husband has a heart condition, my football team is under investigation and my pretty little girl, the best uh-oh that ever happened to me, is pregnant. It's all going away and I just want it back."

"No, Ma. You can't have it back. You have to face yourself now—the person you are without Pop and the team and your daughters to hide behind." Martha watched fresh tears flood her mother's eyes. "We're all still here. We're in your life, but we aren't your life. My life includes this baby and it includes Avery. Accept that."

Tem's mouth fell open. "I thought it was Danica, but… it's you. I see myself in you, Martha."

"I wouldn't manipulate my children."

"No." Wistfully, Tem smiled and took the untouched glass of milk, reclaiming her chair and returning to her solitude. "You'll be a different kind of mother. That's what makes you, *you*, and not me."

Martha went upstairs to her father's office as Joaquin and one of her father's corporate attorneys were leaving. Joaquin stopped, waited until the other man had walked away, then said to her, "I'm not one of Tem's favorite people right now. Or Marshall's, for that matter. But business—"

"Is business. I know. You're supposed to pick and choose your battles, not mine." Martha brushed a fingertip over the cuff of his shirt. "Thanks, though."

"I love you. Your battles are mine."

"Stop saying that. I swear, it hurts to think about you loving me and knowing we can't do anything about it." Touching him, letting him wrap her up in his strength, would only deepen and intensify the hurt.

She hugged him, pressing as close as she could. "We can't talk this out today."

"But we need to, before the fight."

"Yeah."

"Do something for me, Martha. Stay away from the gym for a while. Something's not right with my uncle, and I need to figure out what."

"You sound more like you already know what, and you don't like it."

"A guess. Swear I hope I'm wrong."

Dropping her arms, she let the man she loved go, and entered the office. "Does your cardiac nurse know you're jumping back into work before you've even cut off your patient bracelet, Pop?"

Marshall looked remarkably less exhausted than his wife. He grabbed a pair of scissors from a desk drawer and pulled up his sleeve to snip the bracelet. "Feeling all right, Martha?"

"Ma told you I'm pregnant?"

"So did your sisters, who begged me to not cut you out of the family." With a swish, the blades severed the brace-let. "So did Joaquin, who asked me to not cut you from the publicity department."

"I don't want the publicity department. I want the front office. Someday, I'll prove I belong there."

"Then you'll shake it off."

"Uh…I'm pregnant."

"Shake it off. Mentally. Don't let it get to your head.

It's what I told Joaquin." Marshall set down the scissors, considering. "Want a piece of the corporate world? What about my shares of BC Group?"

"Get some rest, Pop. I'll come back when you're not sedated out of your mind."

"Papers are drawn, for when you want in." He leaned back in his chair, shut his eyes. "Coronary artery spasm. It's a variable I didn't consider. BC Group's pushing for a change, and I need to let the reins go on something. Not my team. That's mine. But I'm rich and risky enough to see what you'll do with shares of BioCures. Together, you and Joaquin would be majority shareholders."

"We're not going to be together. Not in business or anything else."

"What you and he did… There's no way in hell Tem or I can stand by that. But you're going to raise that child without him?"

"It's looking that way. I still want the front office."

"Crawl before you walk, Martha. It's a lesson you'll teach your kid. I haven't decided whether or not I'm going to fire you."

"You're offering me shares of BioCures," Martha said, trying to comprehend the reasoning behind the maneuvers, "but are still considering axing me from the Slayers?"

"Just making assessments. It's what's best for business."

The Las Vegas Slayers had dedicated the NFC championship game to Marshall Blue. Avery, who had never attended a professional sporting event—and never imagined showing up to one in a trendy outfit from the spring collection of a designer whose name was routinely dropped on the red carpet—found herself in a reality she was almost too afraid to believe was hers.

At least, for a little while it was. Discovering a pregnancy test in Martha's house had bluntly put things into perspective. Martha Blue had good intentions and had welcomed her into a life that could've been ripped from a page in Avery's dream-life binder, but Avery would never be part of the Blue family. They were together as a caretaker and foster kid, as friends, on borrowed time. Martha would eventually be sporting a baby bump and making arrangements to extricate Avery from her life.

It had happened before, so Avery knew the drill. She was a temp, a filler.

But it was difficult to remember this, to not get attached to Martha and her family, to resist hugging herself in pure happiness because Martha Blue and Joaquin Ryder had saved her.

Whenever she wanted to be delusional, she pretended that they were in love and would ask her to be a part of their family—not caring that she'd been a crack baby, was short and small for her age and had some emotional scars that resurfaced whenever she started chewing her cuticles until they bled. The cold truth was Joaquin would be leaving after his boxing match, Martha had Complicated Grown-up Stuff that included a pregnancy she was keeping hush-hush and Avery was just a system kid who wasn't meant to belong in anyone's family.

At Slayers Stadium, in the fancytastic owners' box that offered gourmet appetizers and was bustling with people who exuded importance, she was enticed to fall into the delusion again. Martha had brought her to the press box and introduced Avery as her foster daughter, and had sat with her during the pregame fanfare.

During halftime, Martha's mother had pulled her aside to a computer where Marshall Blue had been called on a video conference and when she'd returned to her seat, she'd whispered, "Tem and Marshall asked for my opinion, and she's calling my decision down to the field. Unbelievable."

"They've never asked for your opinion before?"

"No, not regarding strategy. Not as employers seeking

business input from an employee. They *understood* me, Avery. It's what I've wanted for a long time. Understanding."

The game had ended on a clean field goal, and the owners' box had exploded in roars, laughter, champagne and embraces. Tem Blue had grabbed Martha in a hug and Martha had pulled Avery into it, as well. And then it was the three of them joyful in the chaos, until photographers broke them up.

"Chickadee, do you think you could get used to this craziness?"

Avery had looked up at Martha, all the racket rendering her brain a little slow to catch up. "You mean I can come back here?"

"Well, the Slayers' next stop is the Super Bowl, but after that, absolutely. Because the owners' box is always open to family."

Family... The idea that Avery could actually be more than a system kid—but part of a family—left her so giddy that hours later, when Martha finally took her away from the celebration sweeping through Las Vegas, she was still feeling floaty and light and secure.

And wistful, because she thought about Renata now more than she had since running from the condo. She loved Renata for giving her a home and an education in cooking. She hated that cancer had weakened her, and that her creep of a son had taken advantage. But Renata was not her family, maybe because she'd never referred to Avery as family in all their years together.

Voices lured her downstairs after midnight. With Rabbit twitching and sniffing, bundled in her arms, Avery moved quietly in her bare feet. Perhaps it was because every room in Martha's fairy-tale mansion had a locking door, or because she was clued in enough to know Avery needed space and privacy, but for several nights Avery had felt safe enough to go to bed without her shoes on...and dream.

Tiptoeing toward a broad column that divided the open main floor space into two distinct rooms, Avery peeked around it and saw Martha leading Joaquin Ryder to the living room.

"Nothing's changed," Martha said. "You're not going to throw the fight. You're going to win that fight and go to Miami without me."

"Why can't we bend or sacrifice?" Joaquin rested a hand on Martha's stomach. "Why can't we take that kind of risk?"

"Because that kind of risk isn't best for this baby. Either I'll resent you each time you take on a fight or you'll resent me for convincing you to give it up. Can't do that to myself or you or my kids."

Avery gasped, but it made no sound. *Kids.* Instinct said to be thrilled, but it seemed as if Joaquin and Martha were about to walk away from what made them happy.

"Slow dance with me, Martha. That's something I can give you tonight."

"Okay."

Then both were looking at a smartphone and as he scrolled, she said, "Not that one. Keep going." When they seemed to be in agreement, he tapped the phone and jazz music lifted into the air.

Soundlessly kissing Rabbit's forehead, Avery watched the boxer and the math geek heiress tutor who'd rescued her embrace in front of the winter tree. Not speaking, not laughing, they swayed together.

She didn't move until the dancing stopped and the two walked off to the foyer. Hoisting Rabbit to the crook of one elbow, she grabbed a piece of paper, a pen and a ribbon to thread through it. No way was she delusional now. No way was she wrong.

Jotting *love* on the paper, she hung it on a branch and dashed upstairs.

* * *

The televised coverage of the Ryder vs. Brazda weigh-in at the Garden dominated local news and ESPN. After taking to the scales and staring down Eliáš Brazda for several thousand people filling the arena, Joaquin wasn't interested in watching it when he arrived at the steakhouse inside the Rio and glimpsed the video streaming on his cousin's phone.

Today he was going to fire his trainer. At dawn he'd shown up at the gym for a workout to find Jules dismantling his office. He wouldn't say what he was searching for and his pupils had been dilated. As if he'd recently taken a hit of something and was after a refresher. After Joaquin had demanded an explanation about the heavy bag that still hadn't been replaced, Jules had zipped out of the parking lot before Joaquin could stop him.

Jules, who'd seen the damage drugs had done to his sister, who'd rescued Joaquin from that certain fate by putting gloves on him and giving him a way out, was far down the same damn path.

"Can't hype this event more than that," Othello said, turning his phone to give Joaquin a clear view of the screen. "Ready for Saturday?"

"Othello, talk to me about your dad."

Othello put the phone away. "What about him?"

"I know what he's doing at the gym. My eyes were closed to it. But yours weren't. You've known."

"He gets effed up in the office. That gym ain't what it's supposed to be about." Othello picked up his glass for a swallow of iced water. "What it used to be about."

Othello's comment about burning the gym to the ground came surging forward in Joaquin's mind. Get rid of the gym, get his father back. "This thing with Ciera aside, Othello, we need to talk to Tor and make some changes. Jules isn't coming to MGM Grand tomorrow night."

"He's your trainer."

"Not the way he is now. I can't have him in my corner like that. We need to get him help. Can I count on you and Tor to have my back on Saturday?"

Othello frowned. "He's not going to appreciate getting pushed out of the picture."

"Maybe he'll appreciate not ending up like my mother. If not, too freakin' bad. His boys need to come together and save him and his gym—because he saved all of us. Sure as hell saved me."

Martha was going to tell him tonight.

Seduced by the hope in the atmosphere and the spirit of celebration in the city that still lingered almost a week after the Slayers secured a spot in the Super Bowl, she refused to leave MGM Grand on fight night still harboring lies. Assuming that pushing through everyone to get to Joaquin before the main-card fight would only screw with his head, she prepared to watch twelve rounds and afterward would put everything out there.

She had to find out if there was any other choice than to let him go for love.

Yet those best-laid plans were scrapped when her cell phone buzzed midmorning.

I want to see you in a place where we can both be honest.

Accepting a sleek, luxury-car escort to the location where she agreed to meet Joaquin, she found Ryder's Boxing Club heavily secured and closed to the public. Tonight the gym would open as a watch party venue for the neighborhood to enjoy the entire pay-per-view event free of charge. It was a tradition she'd been glad to hear wouldn't be altered in the aftermath of Joaquin firing his uncle as trainer.

A bodyguard opened the door to her and stepped outside when she entered. She walked farther into the sunlight-dappled building and halted several feet from Joaquin, who sat on a set of ringside steps. His clothing simplified to jeans, a cotton shirt and a pair of sunglasses, he was total intensity and strength and ease.

How could he gamble his career on a single match and sit there so casually?

Joaquin held out a hand and she advanced until his palm was cupping her cheek. In his sunglasses she saw her earnest reflection.

"I heard about Jules and the trainer change. I'm sorry he's going through that."

The only indication that he'd absorbed her words was a subtle twitch of his lips. Then, "You're beautiful, Martha."

She took away the sunglasses, hooking them on the neckline of his shirt, combing the depths of his solemn dark irises. It hadn't been a restful night, and she'd awakened early nervous about the fight and what choice she might make afterward. "Say it again."

His fingers barely brushed the delicate, puffy skin under her eyes, then traveled to the corners of her frowning mouth. "Martha, you are beautiful." Not stopping there, he agilely climbed into the ring and helped her onto the canvas. "You're so beautiful. In this square, we don't lie. That's why we're here."

She ran a hand along the top rope as she walked. "Every time we're in this ring, we get overtaken." Letting go, she met him in the center of the square. "We can't this time."

"The pregnancy."

"No, I meant you. Save your energy for the fight."

Joaquin grinned, and there was the dimple in his cheek. "Okay." His fingertips brushed down her spine, lingered on the curve of her ass, and she wanted to keep him there. "And after the fight?"

"After the fight, I'll be squirmy about your bruised face and battered body." This time she smiled, but it quickly fell. "After the fight, we're supposed to be done."

"We're going to choose now to stick to the lines in the sand?"

She shrugged. But there were no lines anymore. There was an unborn child. There was love. "So this is our honest place. This boxing ring."

"'No lies, no bullshit,'" he quoted. "I wanted you to be standing on this canvas with me when I told you that I'm not going to throw this fight. I can't give Brazda a freebie. Above that, my kid needs a father with integrity."

Martha nodded—or she tried to. Respect for his decision combated dread. In her heart, she believed he would outclass Brazda. Then the goodbyes would come. "Okay. My turn to be honest." She glided a palm down his arm. She could touch him, study him, for hours. "I'm not going to hate you for choosing the fight, Joaquin. In fact, I love you. And I feel really good about being the one you gave your trust virginity to."

"Is that so?"

"So."

"So…" He turned and somehow maneuvered her against the ropes. "Make an honest man out of me. Upgrade me from 'guest' to 'groom' at your wedding."

Martha gave a shove. "That's not funny. Asking me to marry you when you're about to fight your way out of my life?"

"I said I'm not throwing this match, Martha. I didn't say there would be more." Joaquin shook his head. "After this event, I'm retiring. I decide whose challenges I accept, and I decide when I'm done searching the ring for the meaning of my life."

"Do not retire for me."

"I'm retiring because what I want isn't at the end of a championship anymore. My place in this sport doesn't mean what it used to. Not to my uncle, and for damn sure not to me anymore. I took on Brazda because I didn't have a reason to stop getting in the ring." Joaquin's touch was warm, comforting on her belly. "This baby's my reason. You're my reason. I'm not the machine…not the beast. That's my reason."

Martha swayed into his arms. Let the scandals begin. If loving Joaquin Ryder was a scandal, then she was thoroughly, shamelessly, dirtily scandalous.

"I'm still nobody's fairy tale. I'm just a man."

"Thank God." So complicated, so difficult, so hard to understand, he would fit perfectly in her unconventional, out-of-order family. *Someone to love and someone who loves me.* Martha smiled against his mouth. "Kiss me, champ."

* * * * *

*Don't miss Lisa Marie Perry's next romance
from* THE BLUE DYNASTY *series,
MINE TONIGHT,
available April 2015 from Kimani Romance!*

REQUEST YOUR FREE BOOKS!

2 FREE NOVELS
PLUS 2 FREE GIFTS!

KIMANI™
ROMANCE

Love's ultimate destination!